BLUE 2...BALE OUT!

LEIF HAMRE

Blue Two ... Bale Out!

Translated from the Norwegian by
EVELYN RAMSDEN

Illustrated by
ARNE JOHNSON

THE CHILDREN'S BOOK CLUB
121 CHARING CROSS ROAD
LONDON W.C.2

First published in Norway in 1958
*by H. Aschehoug & Co. (W. Nygaard), Oslo
under the title "Blå 2—Hopp Ut"*

This edition first published in 1961

English Translation © 1960
*by University of London Press Ltd
and Leif Hamre*

This book was awarded the Norwegian State Prize
for the best children's book of the year

*This edition by arrangement with
University of London Press Ltd*

*Printed in Great Britain by Richard Clay and Company, Ltd.,
Bungay, Suffolk*

Contents

CHAPTER ONE

A Near Shave

———

EARLY in the spring a southerly wind had begun to drive warm Atlantic air in over the coast of Norway. The snow had melted early and the willow branches were covered with bursting catkins even before April was well under way. Almost every morning people woke to find the sun shining in through their windows.

On such a spring morning two jet aircraft were flying low at high speed over the mountains of southern Norway. In the first was 2nd Lieutenant* Peter Hovden and behind him came Lieutenant Geir Grand. Geir was following carefully on the map the route they were to take, while at the same time keeping an eye both on the ground and on the aircraft in front of him. For him the excitement of low-flying was mixed with anxiety, because he had the responsibility of avoiding built-up areas and at the same time keeping a check on Peter, who was flying his first low-level navigation trip. It could hardly be expected that he would get through without making some mistake, however small. When flying at 600 feet a second, a small mistake might soon become a big one.

Peter also realised this. He did not feel altogether confident. Navigation without a map is rather a hopeless affair, and although he had the map-case on his knee he had no

* The Norwegian Air Force uses the same ranks as the British Army.

7

time to look at it. With scarcely 150 feet between him and the ground there was plenty to occupy him outside the cockpit. At the moment he was concentrating on the fact that the next check point should be a lake and that he was due to reach it within seconds. But actually he saw nothing except grey stones and moss in all directions sweeping past below him. Perhaps, for the first time, he wished himself back in the days when he and Geir flew ambulance in the far north of Norway. No doubt in the long run that kind of flying would have been too tame, but the old Otter was a comfortable aircraft and up to no tricks. It kept steadily on and got the job done, although occasionally they had plenty of excitement then too: forced landings in hilly country and in cultivated districts, as well as mountain flying in snowstorms. There had been a little of everything to give colour to everyday life. A crash on the Finnmark moors with Geir was only one among many adventures.

But, but—everyone wanted to go on farther. Everyone dreamt of better aircraft, greater speed, more excitement. First Svein Rowan, their friend who flew helicopters, went to America, where he learnt to fly larger helicopters. When he came home he was appointed head of the Helicopter Section at Rygge. Then Geir went off. He was transferred to jets and stationed at Gardermoen. Within eighteen months he was promoted flight commander—in record time, of course. He was not Geir for nothing.

Well, Bodö became much too dull without either Geir or Svein, and the Otter seemed very tame when Geir's letters praising Thunder Jets had had time to sink in. Then it was jets for Peter too. Jets——? All right, an hour or so a day. Otherwise it meant handbooks and technical orders, piles of handbooks and technical orders, thousands of things to remember, nothing to be forgotten. Hard work, up page and down page, eyes popping out of your head. A

poster in the lecture-room with a burning crashing aircraft and words in fiery red: "He forgot something!"

But where in the world was that blinking lake? He gazed from left to right. Nothing but mountainous country and bare rocks to be seen. But wasn't there a valley cutting straight across the course a little farther on? He glanced quickly down at the map and then up again. Yes, the track really did cross a valley, but not until after the lake had been passed. So he had missed the check point and was out of his course. He looked at the compass. It had not deviated appreciably. No wind either, quite calm, just as the Met. officer had predicted. Should he turn left or right to get on track again? It was pure guesswork anyway. Geir would know,

9

of course. The simplest thing would be to ask him. But— Peter gave a little rueful smile in the midst of his misfortunes. He pictured how Geir would sit solemnly at his desk after the trip and write a very serious and correct report: "Between check points 3 and 4 2nd Lieutenant Hovden lost his track and found himself so-and-so many degrees out of course. The officer had to ask for his position. He should have shown more zeal and initiative and tried to establish his actual position himself. I feel it necessary to report . . ."

"Hi—there's a river in the valley. I ought to be able to find that loop on the map." Peter let go of the throttle and drew his left forefinger along the blue strip on the map.

"Blue 2." Geir's monotonous voice filled the cockpit. "Look out for the ridge across the valley. Climb a little. Over."

"O.K.—climbing. Out." Peter pulled the stick slightly and concentrated on the map again. His forefinger stopped. There was the loop. It looked like a horseshoe with a little curl at the bottom. That agreed with . . .

"PETER—climb! Climb for goodness' sake!"

Peter felt as if his hair were standing on end. He suddenly saw treetops and a black rock close up against the nose of his plane. Quickly he pulled the stick into his stomach and had a total "black-out", staring into pitch-black darkness. Crouched down in his seat and stiff with fright, he waited for the sound of the treetops against the wings.

A moment later he knew he had cleared the trees by a hair's breadth. He pushed the stick forward again and straightened up as the distressing pressure of the centrifugal force diminished. The blood streamed back to his head and the darkness slid away. The instrument board emerged out of grey mist, and his breathing inside the mask was heavy and panting and had a terrified, choking rhythm.

The aircraft banked steeply, and, when he got the first

glimpse of the ground, was almost on its back. A sharp tug at the stick pulled it on to an even keel again, and he emptied his lungs with a sigh of relief. He felt the taste of blood. He had bitten his lips.

The sun dazzled him. The course was wrong; he ought to have had the sun almost at his back. It looked as if it would be an example of a really charming navigation trip! An excellent example of how such a trip should *not* be conducted. A blunder, a—well, well, it was done and could not be undone. But, at any rate, he had to find Geir.

He shook the stick irritably, swung, rose to 1,000 feet and looked around.

Then the earphones clicked.

"Wildcat Blue 2 from Blue leader—course 295 degrees—over."

Peter was on the verge of hysterical laughter. Geir did not waste words. "295 degrees—over." Well, now he knew. Peter checked the compass and cleared his throat before he put his finger on the radio button. "Blue 2 here—I have 295 now. Do you see me? Over."

"Roger—I am 300 feet below you and 2 miles ahead, a little left."

Peter shrugged his shoulders. So, that was that. The exercise had been interrupted. He was to be led home, and taken carefully down to the aerodrome by big brother Geir.

He clenched his teeth, and felt the cut on his lip begin to bleed again. He felt tired and worn out and manoeuvred with restless, violent movements before he got into place behind Geir's wing.

Geir turned and nodded almost imperceptibly. He went into a rising turn and set course for Gardermoen. They pulled down the sun-visors on their helmets.

Without explaining his reason, Geir rose higher and higher. At 12,000 feet he reminded Peter of his oxygen, and

Peter opened the supply pipe to the mask, a little later the pressure valve also.

Only when they reached 20,000 feet did Geir flatten out.

Half of south-eastern Norway lay beneath them in bright sunshine. Their speed was scarcely perceptible any longer. Groups of houses and farms looked like playthings in a modelled landscape. Newly-ploughed fields and meadows clothed in their early green were sharply marked in almost geometrical squares. Ridges covered with dark forests and mountains, still flecked with snow, glided behind them at a snail's pace. Far in front of them the Tyri Fjord and the Rands Fjord gleamed in the sunshine like small patches of water.

Geir kept an eye on Peter's aircraft in his mirror; Peter seemed to be flying carelessly and thoughtlessly. When at last Gardermoen appeared on the horizon like a tiny green field with a grey cross on it, Geir sat undecided for a few moments debating whether he should pull the throttle back for gliding. Then he decided. He turned sharply towards the north. Peter slipped away and remained five yards behind him.

"Hang on!" shrieked Geir into the microphone, quite unnecessarily loudly. Almost at the same moment he went into a tight loop. When he reached the top he shoved the stick forward and let his aircraft continue on its back. In the mirror he saw Peter approach him, and waited until the distance between the wings was three yards. The blood pressed hard against the sockets of his eyes when he went over into a steep dive.

Peter followed. He understood very little of it all, and could scarcely imagine anything more misplaced than aerobatics just now. But if it amused Geir, well, it was all right by him. Low-flying navigation was one thing, aerobatics another. *There* he was quite at home.

He glued his eyes to Geir's wing and kept his distance. The flying became more and more breakneck. He lost almost all feeling of what was happening. The earth and the sun danced round them, sometimes above, sometimes below, sometimes to the right, sometimes to the left. But he hung on. Geir was mistaken if he thought he was going to shake him off. He would hang on, rather nearer for all he cared, two yards perhaps—would that suit? Very well, then—two yards. Or one and a half? The more we are together . . .!

By degrees Peter began to feel in better spirits. The excitement carried him along. His thoughts shot like lightning through his brain, and arms and legs reacted automatically whenever he noticed the smallest alteration in distance between the two wings. He felt he was flying well. The plane answered his swift thoughts as if his nerves radiated to the rudders and the engine through pedals, stick, and throttle. He felt that the plane's enormous powers were his own. He felt them right out to his fingertips. Every fibre in his body was in intimate contact with the plane. He was its master, and felt intensely that it responded to his every desire.

Suddenly the earth and the sun stood still and were in their right place again. Geir had straightened out and went into a shallow dive towards Gardermoen. Only now did Peter realise that the sweat was pouring off him. He shoved his helmet backwards and wiped the perspiration from his eyes. His clothes clung to his body and both arms and legs ached with fatigue.

Geir turned round and looked at him. They were so near to each other that Peter could see a merry twinkle in Geir's eyes blinking at him above the oxygen mask. It really looked as if he were laughing.

The earphones crackled.

"Stop nudging me in the back!" said Geir.

CHAPTER TWO

The Ship's Bell

THE ship's bell which belonged to 317 Squadron was a symbol, a tradition, an almost sacred thing.

Once upon a time it had clanged the departure of a fjord steamer, a small boat which spent its whole life plying up and down a narrow fjord on the west coast of Norway. It signalled departure from at least twenty small wooden quays and had become rusty and cracked by the time its ship was sold as scrap iron and the bell itself by many roundabout ways attained a position of honour and dignity at the entrance to 317 Squadron's station.

For a long time it was just considered a decoration.

But one day it happened that one of the pilots reported to the squadron commander a mistake he had made while landing. As it might easily have ended in a crash, he thought it would be useful both for him and for others if they discussed how such a mistake could be avoided. His squadron commander agreed enthusiastically and wanted to call the pilots together at once, for he made a special point of getting the men to talk freely about their difficulties and problems.

"Call them all together," he said. "Or why not ring the bell? They will guess that something is in the wind."

That was the beginning of the ritual and "law of the bell". From that time on the bell was rung when a pilot had made a mistake in the air or had been exposed to an experience against which he thought his companions ought to be warned. Then he became the "bell-ringer" and had to go through the ritual that was enjoined by "the law of the bell". When he beat a single blow on the bell, all pilots, from the squadron commander to the youngest cadet, were bound to leave whatever jobs they were doing and come to the squadron briefing-room at once. In the meantime the bell-ringer would have unhooked the bell from its place on the wall, brought it with him to the lecture-room, and put it on the desk together with cleaning materials, a brush and polishing cloth. He was considered to be head of the briefing-room as long as the ceremony lasted, and the men saluted him as they came in. As soon as they were all in their places the bell-ringer began to speak. The ritual demanded that he should begin his speech in a special manner:

"Brothers-at-Arms! Fellow Airmen! I am the bell-ringer.

I am responsible for the honourable task of cleaning the bell of 317 Squadron. While doing so I will explain how I attained to this honour, in order to help those who wish to learn a new trade, and to warn those who are content with the profession they are in."

While cleaning the bell he described the experience which had turned him into a bell-ringer. He then called for discussion, which generally ran high. But even if the subject were serious, the gay atmosphere that always prevailed removed the sting from anything approaching criticism. The bell-ringer was carrying out a self-imposed task. Nobody could order him to do it. It was an affair of honour. Therefore they all had a feeling of respect towards the man who stood there alone, acknowledging his fault, in order to warn his comrades against the difficulties into which he had fallen.

The ship's bell had thus become more than a method of teaching bell-ringers to polish brass. It taught the airmen to work together as in a football team. Selfish place-seekers anxious to keep their own experiences to themselves never became bell-ringers; neither did they ever become of great service to 317 Squadron.

The morning after Geir's and Peter's low-flying exercise the two men met in the mess. Geir was just finishing his breakfast when Peter dashed in and dumped himself down beside him. Practically the same routine happened every morning. Geir glanced at his wrist watch, lifted the coffee-pot, and poured them each a cup of coffee. Peter reached for a slice of bread with his left hand, at the same time trying to get butter on his knife with the other.

"Ten minutes," said Geir. "You've almost time to eat all you want."

"Never," groaned Peter with his mouth full. "I shall always go hungry until lunch-time as long as I stay in the Air Force. We begin the day too early."

Geir drank his coffee, pushed his chair a little way from the table, and put his pipe in his mouth. Then he hunted for matches in all his pockets.

"It seems to me that certain things indicate it's you who start too late," he replied.

"Not on your life," puffed Peter. "As a matter of fact, I begin earlier than I should from the point of view of health. Sleep is as important for health as food. The Force should have arranged it so as to give us enough of both."

Geir smiled. His box of matches, which he had found at last, was full of deadheads, and he poked about with his forefinger for a long time before he found an unused one and lighted his pipe. He leant against the back of his chair, pushed his hands deep down into his trouser pockets, and stretched out his legs.

"Our aerobatics yesterday were hard on my nerves," he said.

Peter gave him a quick sideways glance. "Why so?" he asked.

"Oh—you were pretty close, I think. Every moment I expected you to cut off a good slice of my wing."

Peter gulped down some coffee and shrugged his shoulders. "I thought I held the distance well," he said in an injured tone of voice.

"You certainly did. One might have thought you were fully qualified on jets."

Peter met Geir's look with a flash of pleasure in his eyes. But something or other made him avert his eyes and swallow.

"Why were you nervous, then?" he asked.

Geir rose slowly. "There is always danger, nevertheless. It's never a good thing to be *too* sure of oneself."

"Then I can't make out why you allowed me to fly so close?"

Geir did not answer. He began to move towards the door. One of the jeeps outside hooted, and Peter left the last slice of bread and followed him. They emerged into the passage and both of them fetched their caps from the cloakroom.

At the door Peter stopped and took Geir's arm. There was a note of annoyance in his voice when he spoke: "Why did you actually go in for those aerobatics yesterday?" he asked. "I was supposed to be doing a navigation exercise."

Geir thought for a moment. He made a sign to the driver through the glass door and said in passing, as he lifted the latch and went out: "Have you never heard that when a ski-jumper falls he immediately goes right to the top and jumps again? I think it's a good rule to follow."

He went out to the jeep and got in. Peter sat silently beside him as they drove to the briefing-room.

That morning the meeting did not interest Peter particularly. He was not going to fly, and listened with only half an ear to the briefing on the weather, the day's flights, the radio frequencies, and the other things that were always announced at the morning meeting. Neither was Geir going to fly, but he sat there taking notes, nevertheless.

"What are we going to do today?" asked Peter as they left.

"First of all, I've got some reports to write," said Geir. "In the meantime you must have a go at the instructions for blind landing at Sola. We're going to train over there in a couple of days."

"All right! May I sit in your office?"

"Yes, as soon as I'm there alone. The other flight commanders are all going to fly."

Half an hour later the last planes rolled out from the Squadron, and Peter, with the *Pilot's Handbook* under his arm, knocked at the door of the flight commanders' office. Geir was alone. He was sitting at the desk writing.

"Busy?" asked Peter.

"Fairly," answered Geir, pointing to a chair. "But perhaps you can help me. I am writing the report of our trip yesterday."

A watchful look came into Peter's eyes. "Have you any special difficulties there?" he asked.

"Yes—the reason for breaking off the exercise."

"Do you *have* to report that?"

"Have I . . . But we did!"

"But no one else knows."

The moment he had said this Peter could have bitten his tongue off. He blushed to the roots of his hair and searched his brain to find a way out. But he found none. At least not one that would suit Geir. For him there was never more than one way of doing a thing—the correct and unimpeachable way. No doubt a halo would sit firmly on his head one fine day.

Geir held his pen as if he were just about to write, but did nothing beyond staring down at the report-book.

At last he said in a low voice: "We broke off the exercise. You haven't carried it through. So you must do it again."

"It was *you* who broke it off, not *we*," said Peter, searching restlessly for a usable argument. "I could just as well have continued the navigation exercise as follow you in those breakneck aerobatics."

"I wanted to give you time to pull yourself together."

"Did you know how long I needed?"

Geir shrugged his shoulders. "I guessed, but of course I did not actually know."

"Couldn't you have asked me?"

"Did you know yourself?"

"Of course I did. I was O.K. and I could have gone on at once."

"Well——"

But Peter would not give in. He was furious because he had made a fool of himself. But he was also angry with Geir because he was so unshakeable once he had come to a conclusion.

"The question is whether it was correct to break off without so much as asking me if I was O.K.," he said angrily.

Geir's face darkened. He threw his pen down on the table abruptly, and a cold gleam came into his eyes.

"Who is the flight commander?" he rapped out. "You or I? I thought it was *I* to whom an explanation was due, but you seem to think it is to *you*."

He jumped up and leant across towards Peter, his hands planted palms downwards on the table.

"And you shall have an explanation which you did not expect," he went on. "When you pulled up and cleared the ridge you did not see me. I, on the other hand, got a close-up view which I wish I hadn't had. You pulled the aircraft up and to the right without thinking that I was just behind you, slightly higher and a little to the right of you. As we passed one another we were just about as close to each other as you had been to the ridge a moment before. My shock was as great as yours. I had no wish to go on with the low flying and had no grounds for thinking that you had either."

Peter had grown very pale. He stared at the toecaps of his boots and clenched his hands. The room became very quiet for a moment.

"I didn't realise that," said Peter at last.

"No, it wasn't easy for you to discover," answered Geir in a milder tone of voice. "But that was what I had thought we might discuss."

Peter swallowed. "It was a pity you didn't tell me before I made such a fool of myself," he said thickly. "I am— am——"

Suddenly a gleam came into his eyes and his face assumed an almost gay expression.

"I am—a bell-ringer," he burst out. "That's what I am—a bell-ringer——!"

"You'll get the cleaning materials from the adjutant," said Geir calmly.

CHAPTER THREE

317 Squadron

IN its own eyes 317 Squadron was the world's best squadron. Of course they had no real proof of this, but then they had no proof to the contrary either. Their training results had been the best in the Norwegian Air Force for several years running, and pilots as well as mechanics were all ready to share their good or bad luck with each other in order to keep up the squadron's reputation. This welded them together into a comradeship where everyone who did a job, whether in the air or on the ground, were equally important members of the team.

The hangar and the dispersal hut were half hidden among trees at the foot of a little rock called Gardefjell. There the forest had been cut down to form a big square. In the daytime the aircraft were parked on the tarmac in front of the hangar. When going out they went along a broad concrete strip to the perimeter track which encircled the whole airfield.

The squadron commander, the technical officer, and the flight commanders had their offices in the dispersal hut. The squadron's briefing-room, in which meetings and discussions were held, was also there. The pilots usually occupied it when they were not flying or had no other reasons for being elsewhere. The walls were covered with notice-boards containing such information as weather reports, lists of flights, training results, times of departure, and landing times. In one corner there was a small library of technical handbooks, instructions, and orders. Almost every day a new book was added that the boys had to read.

The squadron commander, Major Tangen, was a tall, broad-shouldered man with pronounced features and an energetic face. His nose was beaked like an Indian's, and his chin stuck out almost as far as his nose. It was said he breathed through it when flying on his back. Everybody found it natural and right that Major Tangen should be in command. He was an outstanding pilot and a real master of all trades, but also a comrade known affectionately by many names, of which the Major, the Chief, the Boss, the Governor, the Old Man, and "he himself" were the most common.

Captain Robertsen, whose forty years made him the oldest man in the squadron, held sway in the hangars. He had been a mechanic during the war, and wore ribbons above his breast-pocket. Generally they were hidden beneath a greasy overall which was Robertsen's favourite garment. He regarded uniforms simply as underclothes. Anybody who wanted to talk to Robertsen about engines and motors needed plenty of time to spare. There was no chance of getting away except by standing near the door and slipping out when Robertsen paused to draw breath. He would have been bored to death in a community where there were no engines. The more troublesome his engines were, the more he loved them, and the more tenderly he nursed and cured them. The boys called him the "Motor-doctor" or simply "Doc". Occasionally, of course, he had to sit in his office, but if engines were working outside he never finished his office work. He would listen intently for suspicious sounds and make his diagnosis. It had happened—at least rumours said so—that he once opened the window and shouted: "For heaven's sake, are you going to drive me crazy? Can't you hear that the nozzle must be replaced in combustion-chamber eight?"

The four flight commanders were all younger men. They had been chosen because they were energetic and good leaders. Geir, who led D-Flight, was the youngest. "Well, yes, on the surface," said the boys, "but inside he is at least as old as the others."

Peter flew as No. 2 in D-Flight. Neither he nor Geir had changed much since they were rescued after the crash with the Otter on the Finnmark plain a few years ago. They were close friends, although they were so different in temperament and looks, or perhaps for that very reason. Geir's calm, thoughtful nature needed perhaps, in order to develop fully, the contact with Peter's impulsive, volatile, and almost mischievous turn of mind. And the converse was, no doubt, also true. Neither of them had felt completely happy during the time they had been separated.

But D-Flight had two other airmen—excellent pilots and good chaps, too: Torbjørn Nygård and Terje Ness.

Torbjørn was most easily recognised by the fact that he always had his hands in his pockets. He was tall and thin, with lively, glaringly blue, eyes. His body seemed to consist mainly of bones, muscles, and sinews. As a rule his muscles were quite relaxed, but when he felt inclined he could use them to good effect; for instance, to run the hundred yards in eleven seconds or do a high jump of almost six feet. Unfortunately, it was only seldom he exerted himself to that extent.

Torbjørn's face was narrow and full of laughter-lines, and was placed at the top of a long, crane-like neck with an incredibly large Adam's apple. His collar always looked as if it were two sizes too large for him, and his cap had to be specially made in a child's size. But knowledge apparently takes up very little room, for the small knob on which Torbjørn's cap was perched was full of all sorts of wisdom learnt from what he had heard and seen. He knew everything worth knowing about flying, and yet he was seldom seen to open a book. It seemed that all he needed was to read the title. Then he would know what was inside the book.

Torbjørn was the prodigy of 317, a man who stormed the heights without apparently knowing what opposition or difficulties meant. He was master of the situation both in the air and on the ground. Yet there was no one who exerted himself less than he did.

It was a very different matter with Terje. He was the youngest of the four, modest and gentle, a mere stripling who didn't appear to have either the health or the strength to fly jets. But appearances are often deceptive. Behind the soft, boyish face was hidden an indomitable will which had only one object in view—to be as good a pilot as the others. On the ground Terje looked like a boy who had borrowed flying-clothes from a grown-up man, and his voice was thin and hesitating. But in the air nothing but his helmet was visible and his voice was as firm and incisive as the voice of anyone else.

D-Flight was a four-leaved clover. The four men were much like other airmen. They had their peculiarities, their faults, and their virtues, but on the job they pulled together like horses in a four-in-hand.

One day, at the end of May, summer came in with a rush. The buds on the trees bust open, the birches stood round the hangars in all their spring splendour, and the air was full of the smell of fresh leaves and damp grass. A dirty heap of snow that lay along the north side of the hangar was fast diminishing, and the concrete was dry, and had a clean, newly-scrubbed look.

After a training flight in the morning D-Flight taxied on to the tarmac and parked. The pilots switched off the engines and left the planes to the mechanics. They all walked slowly

25

in a group towards their quarters, with their parachutes and rubber dinghies slung over their shoulders.

"Let's stay out in the sun for a while," said Terje. He pulled off his helmet and sniffed the air.

"Right!" said Torbjørn. "Let's sit down on those boxes by the hangar. O.K., Chief?"

Geir nodded and glanced at his wrist watch. "I'll join you as soon as I've written my report," he said. "There's almost an hour before lunch."

They settled themselves down on the boxes, and Torbjørn lit a cigarette. The flies hummed on the wall behind them, and the warm, sweet smell of the pines reached them from the forest at their backs.

"The spring," said Torbjørn theatrically, throwing out his arms towards the sun—"the spring, gentlemen, makes me feel quite lyrical. The spring is like a—a dry nappy on a wet . . . a wet happy-tappy."

"What's a 'happy-tappy'?" asked Peter, laughing.

"Oh, nothing in particular—it just rhymes with 'nappy' and it means anything you like to make it mean. In surrealist poetry you can change the meaning according to your mood and inclination."

"I thought it was a poet's job to put a meaning into anything he wrote," said Peter.

"That's because you have no feeling for modern poetry," retorted Torbjørn. "You probably like naturalism better!"

Peter shook his head.

"Depends on the poetry," he said. "Have you any examples of your own so-called naturalistic poetry?"

"Well, actually," said Torbjørn, "I've finished even with naturalism a long time ago. I go in for free verse nowadays."

"Give us one about spring. It's the sort of thing all poets write about."

26

"I can't remember one about spring, but I once wrote one about winter."

"Oh, any season will do," cried Peter.

Torbjørn put his head on one side and thought. Then he lifted his arms towards an imaginary audience and declaimed:

> "The ski-tracks wind among the trees,
> With skiers crawling on their knees.
> They look just like emergencies,
> But they're only tourists from overseas."

His audience shrieked with laughter and Peter said, "What a pity that a poet like you should waste his time flying!"

As the lunch hour approached many planes came in to land and the men had to raise and lower their voices according to the noise of the engines. Suddenly, from afar, they heard a steady hum and a rattling noise which gradually grew stronger.

"Evidently we're in for a visit from one of the Mixmasters from Rygge," remarked Terje, after he had been listening for a time.

"That's right," said Torbjørn. "Perhaps it's our dear friend Svein."

"Hope so," said Peter.

The helicopter approached in a shallow glide and came right across the aerodrome. It headed towards the platform in front of the control tower, and disappeared from sight behind the trees. They heard the engine running while the helicopter stood on the ground. A little later the roar began again, the noise approached, and the strange dragonfly appeared over the treetops fifty yards away.

It was easy to see that it was Svein. His enormous bulk seemed to fill the whole cockpit. He made a sharp turn over the roof of the hangar, descended almost perpendicularly to

27

the platform, and stopped short about a yard from the ground.

Jet pilots always have their hearts in their mouths as they watch a helicopter land. The manoeuvre seems so absolutely against nature that they can hardly believe it can be made successfully. Peter jumped down from the boxes, and the others followed suit. The current of air from the rotor swept towards them along the ground and forced them to turn round and wait until the noise of the engine died away. But the rotor still hummed its warning "shuitt, shuitt", keeping everyone at a safe distance.

Svein opened the door, grinning: "Is an ordinary human being allowed to set foot on the sacred precincts of 317?" His strong voice boomed out over the squadron area, and busy mechanics rummaging in the engines with their behinds in the air jumped and looked round.

"That voice will go right through the sound barrier one of these days," remarked Torbjørn drily.

Peter clicked his heels together. "It's an honour, sir," he shouted jokingly to Svein. "Anyway, haven't you been given free and unrestricted access to our territory long ago?"

"Right!" roared Svein. "But I must point out that the concrete was at that time covered with snow!"

"Makes not the slightest difference," laughed Peter. "Snow or concrete, it's all ours, and yours when you are our guest. Get out and make yourself at home. The red carpet is unfortunately at the cleaners."

Torbjørn, ducking beneath the rotor, went forward to the cockpit door and held it open. "I have always wondered how in the world you get through that little hole," he said to Svein. "It's a performance for which I have the very greatest respect."

"You flatter me," said Svein. He turned with his back

28

towards them and stuck his long legs through the door. For a moment his huge form filled every inch of the opening, but out he came, apparently without the slightest difficulty.

"Incredible!" said Torbjørn. "If you took a larger size in boots the door would have to be enlarged. Do you dare to eat anything when you are once in there?"

Svein ignored the question, thumping Peter's shoulder so heavily that his knees knocked together. Then he shouted, "How are you?"

"Fine," said Peter; "and you?"

"Bad, very bad. Symptoms of appendicitis. I've lost almost a stone."

"A stone for you is nothing," scoffed Terje. "It corresponds to a couple of ounces with me."

Talking and laughing, they sauntered towards the dispersal hut, where they met Geir and Captain Robertsen, who were on their way out.

"Hi, Svein!" shouted Geir. "Just in time for lunch, as usual. But my goodness, you're getting fat!"

"Wha—?" said Svein, and could not for once think of an answer.

They went in to clean up before leaving for the mess.

But Robertsen did not go in. He wandered over to the helicopter, where he joined a group of mechanics who were studying the strange machine with professional but sceptical interest.

Robertsen took a twist of cotton waste out of his pocket and rubbed it backwards and forwards in the palms of his hands. He had only just washed them, but the cotton waste gave them by degrees a grey, greasy look. Robertsen could never think properly without rubbing a twist of cotton waste between his hands, and now he was thinking hard.

A young sergeant standing beside him said, "A strange sort of aircraft, isn't it, Captain?"

"Isn't an aircraft at all," said Robertsen sulkily.

"Well, no, that's true enough; but it flies——"

"Flies? That thing? It can't fly?"

"But I've seen it fly."

Robertsen shrugged his shoulders disdainfully and glanced disapprovingly at the sergeant.

"When you're as old as I am, my boy," he said slowly, "you won't believe everything you see."

CHAPTER FOUR

Bale Out!

CONDENSATION trails marked their track. Sixteen strips widened behind them and converged in a long, narrow cloud. The whole squadron was flying in closed formation.

The air was crystal-clear. Above them the sky was a greenish blue, an almost luminous colour, turning into a deeper blue down by the horizon. The sun gleamed on the perspex and the wings. But the ground was hidden beneath a monotonous, greyish-white carpet of cloud which from that great height looked almost flat.

There was not a sound on the radio. They kept a steady course homewards—towards the south—with the sun in their faces. Peter sat relaxed in his seat, keeping the tip of Geir's wing in the corner of his eye. He was farthest to the left in the formation. The other aircraft looked as if they were standing still, as if hanging from invisible threads and just rocking a little out of rhythm. They had been flying thus for so long that the monotonous humming from the engines was almost like silence. It made him drowsy. It had an unreal, sleep-inducing undertone which separated him more and more from consciousness.

Suddenly the flyers heard a resounding, excited voice in their earphones.

"Wildcat Blue 2 from Blue 4—What is the matter?—Over." It was Terje's voice.

Geir started. He turned his head and looked anxiously at Peter's plane. It was flying close to his wing and pitched uneasily up and down in a sort of even, rhythmic, snake-like movement. The white helmet in the cockpit followed the rhythm, as if Peter were unable to carry its weight any longer.

Lack of oxygen! The thought leapt through Geir's brain. A cold shiver ran down his spine and he had gooseflesh all over his body. It was impossible to mistake the symptoms. Peter was only half conscious. It was his pulse that made him pull and slacken the stick a millimetre or two every time his heart beat.

Geir's fingers were shaking when he pushed the radio button. "Check oxygen, Blue 2, check oxygen! Over."

He could see that Peter did not react. His head waggled helplessly and his plane had begun to drift slowly but surely out of formation.

"Blue 2—Peter—do you hear me? Set oxygen at 100 per cent."

A slight reaction, a dull, unintelligible answer, a low mumble, but the aircraft continued to drift away.

"Wake up, Peter! Pull yourself together! Wake up! Check oxygen. Check oxygen!"

No answer.

The squadron commander broke in and gave a quick order to Geir: "Blue 1 from Wildcat leader—follow him—over."

"Understood—Blue 1 out."

Geir slackened speed a shade to let Peter overtake him. The rest of the squadron rose a few hundred feet, and Geir was left alone with the responsibility of a pilotless plane on his hands—with Peter on board. What should he do? Shout? Shriek? Force himself into Peter's consciousness trying to get him to react instinctively? Oh, it was all no use. He was powerless. He was shouting to ears that could not hear.

Nothing would be any good until they came down to denser air containing more oxygen. But what else could he do now? Nothing!

He glanced at the vertical speed indicator. They were sinking a little, barely noticeably. The altimeter showed 24,000 feet and every moment was pushing Peter deeper into unconsciousness. They must go down more quickly, more quickly to dense, life-giving air which would clear Peter's brain. But then——? No, not too fast either. Not so quickly that they crashed before Peter regained consciousness.

The diving angle became a little steeper. The pace increased. Geir kept ten yards from Peter's plane. He saw that his head had fallen forward, his chin resting on his chest. The rhythmic pitching had ceased. He must have let go of the stick. Fate was now in command.

C

Twenty-three thousand feet. Was fate searching for a suitable diving angle? For a golden mean?

Everything depended on how great was the fault in the oxygen system—a leak, a displacement of the mask, or complete failure. If the supply of oxygen had not been completely stopped, the air a few thousand feet lower would perhaps give Peter the surplus that was necessary. There was otherwise just a microscopic chance that he would wake in time. Or none——

"Jump, Peter! Jump!"

The needle of the vertical speed indicator continued to sink. The altimeter revolved quicker. The noses of the two aircraft dug down towards the carpet of clouds. Quicker and quicker.

Twenty-one thousand.

"Bale out!"

Twenty thousand.

"Jump! Bale out!"

Nineteen thousand—no, eighteen thousand.

Geir was lost to the world around him. The only things that existed for him were his own cockpit and Peter's aircraft with the white helmet behind the triplex glass.

"Peter, Peter! Get out!"

By now the fog in Peter's brain must have begun to disperse. The words must be penetrating and gaining a meaning little by little. If only he could hammer the thought into Peter's brain that he must get out of the plane, he would instinctively know what to do, even if he were not fully conscious. A firm grip on the ejection handle was all that was necessary. The seat would be shot right through the perspex and the automatic barometer release would open the seat belt and release the parachute.

"Jump out! Jump out!"

Fifteen thousand feet. The aircraft were now plunging almost perpendicularly. The clouds rushed towards them. The needle on the mach-meter leaped forward in small jumps and passed mach 0·8—eight-tenths of the velocity of sound. It approached the red line which showed the limit of what the aircraft could stand. The noise from the motor and the flame changed its character. He heard the sound of Peter's plane above his own. As they approached the sound barrier only a low, growling, almost a whisper, reached the cockpit.

"Peter . . .!"

A violent, shattering vibration suddenly shook the plane, as when a bicycle tyre explodes on a stony road. Shockwaves! The borderlands of the sound barrier! Compact whorls of air against the wings!

Geir's hold on the stick stiffened. His knees trembled so much that his feet almost slipped off the pedals. His body shook in time with the aircraft, so that his instrument panel became a confused blur.

"Close throttles! Dive brakes out!" The vibration increased. The jerks shot like cramp spasms through the fuselage. "Nose up! Slow down before the wings break!" The thoughts flew like streaks of lightning through his brain. But the stick was held firmly as in a vice by the pressure of air against the rudders. He had to drag it towards him with both hands on the handle, his legs braced against the pedals. The jerks became worse and worse. The aircraft butted wildly against the compressed air. The wings! Would they hold? Could they hold? He gave a little. It helped, it helped. He pulled, gave slightly, pulled, gave slightly. Every time there was a little less vibration, a little less precipitous angle, a little less speed. But the clouds came towards him like a wall. The height was scarcely 12,000 feet. Now it was a case of holding or bursting. He pulled the stick with all his might. A series of blows as from a steamhammer against the wings threw him resistlessly round in the cockpit—and then, just as suddenly as it had begun, it was over. The aircraft slipped through the air like a ship on a smooth sea and he heard his own breath gushing in and out of the mask in a panting, gasping rhythm.

"PETER! BALE OUT! PETER! BALE OUT!"

The clouds closed together round him. His eyes glided quickly over the artificial horizon on the instrument panel. The little aircraft silhouette inside the glass mounted towards the white horizon line. But just before it got so far he shoved the stick forward and swung in a wide left turn towards the ground, shouting all the time.

Peter was fighting against a disagreeable feeling that somebody was holding his shoulders in an iron grip, shaking him violently back and forth. His head swung powerlessly and banged incessantly against something or other. At the same time someone was shouting into his ear, but it was an unintelligible, meaningless shout. He turned away and tried to open his eyes, to see who it was that was plaguing him. With a tremendous effort he got them half-open, but everything around him danced in a wild witches' dance. He could not fix his gaze steadily on any one thing.

There was the voice again, grating and jarring in his ear. A shout, a bawl without meaning.

He got hold of something with one hand, and held on to it tightly. He tried to keep his head steady and half opened his eyes again. In front of him danced a grey shadow with white circles in it. Somewhere or other a red lamp shone and drew confusing lines and figures. Nothing stood still. All was noise and confusion around him. It howled and piped and rattled. He was surrounded by an inferno of howling, whistling, creaking, hammering noises.

Just one clear thought cut like a blinding gleam of light

36

into his consciousness. The engine—the engine—he was flying. Good lord! he was flying!

He opened his eyes wide and clung with both hands to whatever he could get hold of. Unconsciously his hand tightened round the quivering stick. The other gripped the throttle and his feet fumbled for the pedals. His eyes stared at the shaking instrument panel without realising what the indicators showed. Outside the perspex stood a wall of impenetrable fog.

Suddenly he rushed perpendicularly out of the cloud. The ground rose in front of him like a wall, trembling, heaving, gleaming like an out-worn piece of film. He felt a tight grip on his throat—a heavy blow in the midriff—he gasped for breath, he panted, groaned, threw himself forward in his shoulder-straps, grasped the stick with both hands, and pulled it towards him with his legs convulsively tensed against the pedals. A long-drawn-out, hollow cry of terror rang wildly in his ears, and he was only half conscious that it was through his own clenched teeth that the sound had come.

The stick did not move.

"PETER! BALE OUT!" Geir's voice filled the cockpit and drowned the noise from outside.

Peter's grip on the stick loosened. As if in a dream he made his preparations, without confusion, without undue haste—exactly as he had practised them and thought them out a thousand times. He straightened his back, drew his legs in, leant his head against the backrest, grasped the handle of the discharging mechanism, and pulled it.

Confusedly he sensed a sharp bang, a tug, a thump on his helmet, and the paralysing blow, as if he had been thrown against a wall, when he met the violent air pressure outside the plane. It knocked the air out of him, and almost pulled his shoulders and hips out of joint. In a few moments he almost became unconscious again. He did not notice when the barometer release severed him from the chair and released the parachute. When his brain eventually cleared enough for him to know what was happening, he was dangling violently in the strings a few yards from the ground. He had just time to bend his knees and brace his muscles to receive the shock of landing.

Happily he landed in a field of long, soft grass. He was thrown down brutally, and lay for a long time on his back, quite apathetic, panting as if after an exhausting run. His whole body ached. He felt as if he had been soundly drugged and was almost at his last gasp.

A plane suddenly came out of the clouds and passed him, flying low.

With an effort Peter dragged himself wearily to his feet. His legs held. He could stand. He could also use his arms. Nothing was broken. Incredible as it might seem, he had come through without any damage done. He pulled off his helmet and threw it to the ground.

The aircraft returned. He saw it was Geir. It glided straight at him, waved its wings, passed him, rose, and made off through the clouds.

Peter had not waved. He stood there, his shoulders sagging, looking dully in the direction in which the plane had disappeared. His head was aching badly.

The wreck of his own aircraft lay on fire about three hundred yards away. The flames rose high into the air, and a black pillar of smoke drifted among the trees of a small wood.

A little muscle in his chin vibrated incessantly and he pressed his hand against it to keep it still.

People came running towards him from a nearby farm.

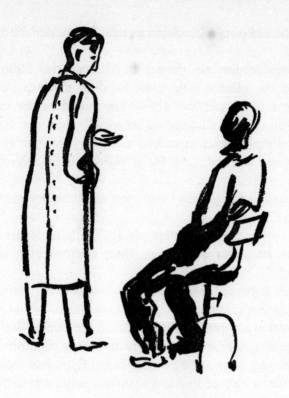

CHAPTER FIVE

Grounded

SCARCELY an hour later Peter was in the air again, in the helicopter that had come to fetch him. Tired and worn out, he sat in the corner beside the pilot as they flew low along the Mjøsa Lake towards the south. The water below them was like glass, and there was not a breath of wind in the air.

The pilot said something to Peter which he did not take

in. As he did not feel inclined to talk, he nodded, and left it at that.

"I was in the air—heard it all over the radio——" shouted the pilot a little later, bending towards Peter so that he might hear him above the sound of the engine. "Amazing that it all went off so well."

Unwillingly Peter stretched out his hand for the earphones and put them on. He straightened the microphone a little.

"What did Lieutenant Grand say when he saw me on the ground?"

The pilot laughed. "He said: 'Wildcat leader from Blue 1. Bale out successful. Blue 2 apparently unhurt. Over.'"

Peter answered nothing. The corners of his mouth trembled in a slight smile.

"It was really rather comical," said the pilot. "We sat on tenterhooks, waiting. The radio had been as quiet as the grave for a minute, and no one thought you had much of a chance. Frankly, we thought that the scream was the end of all things."

"What scream?" Peter felt himself flushing. "What scream?" he repeated.

The pilot looked at him uncertainly. "Yours," he said hesitatingly. He regretted he had mentioned it.

"Did you hear a scream over the radio?"

"Yes."

"When?"

"It must have been just before you jumped."

Peter suddenly felt sick.

He leaned his head on the back of the seat, shut his eyes, and swallowed several times.

"I don't remember it," he stammered. "I tried to get the aircraft out of the dive and must have touched the radio button when I pulled the stick with both hands. But that I screamed—that I cannot remember."

"That isn't at all strange. You were probably only half conscious."

"Yes." Peter shook his head unnecessarily vigorously. "I only remember bits of it all."

They could now see the runway at Gardermoen. The pilot called the control tower and was given permission to land. A little later he said: "I suppose you are to be put down at the hospital?"

"I suppose so," said Peter.

So as to avoid aircraft in the landing circuit they maintained a height of barely two hundred feet for the last miles, and flew a roundabout way to the south of the station. They landed at the side of the taxi-strip, a little way from the hospital.

"Shall I cut the engine and help you out?" asked the pilot.

"No, thank you, I can manage. Thanks for the lift," said Peter. He opened the door, took his helmet and the rolled-up parachute under his arm, and got out. Bent almost double, he emerged from the danger zone of the turning rotor, and tottered stiffly across the grass towards the hospital.

Three men came to meet him: the doctor, Major Tangen, and Geir.

"Good to see you again. How are you?" said Tangen. "No bones broken?"

"I don't think so, sir."

"Fine. If you don't find any yourself, I am sure Dr. Bjerke won't find any either," said the squadron commander with a glance at the doctor. He took the parachute from Peter and gave it to Geir to carry.

"Come along," said the doctor, taking hold of Peter's

41

arm. He held out his free hand for the helmet, but Peter shook his head and kept it.

"Haven't you even a scratch?" asked Geir.

"No. But I am rather stiff. All my joints creak."

"One can be stiff from much less than you have been through," said Tangen. "You almost banged against the sound barrier when you shot into the air. You took a bit of a jolt, I should think."

Peter agreed, with a nod. They had begun to mount the steps, and he felt a pain in his right knee when he lifted it.

"Aren't you limping?" said Dr. Bjerke.

"No, it's only difficult on the steps."

The medical orderly received them, put Peter in a chair, and began to pull off his boots. The doctor hung his jacket on a hook, and put on his white coat. The squadron commander and Geir remained standing in the doorway.

"Come back in an hour's time," said the doctor. "I shan't have finished with him much before that."

It was, however, more than an hour before he had finished with Peter. Dr. Bjerke was a very thorough man. He was about the same age as most of the pilots, but his military service at Gardermoen was his first practice, and he went in for it wholeheartedly. He felt a heavy responsibility for those who were flying, and they on their side considered him as both friend and doctor. They sought his advice on every conceivable disorder, from a cold to failing nerves. No one else on the station, not even the squadron commander, knew so much as he did about the many problems the boys had to face in the air and on the ground.

"Were you frightened?" he asked Peter.

"Yes," said Peter.

"Are you nervous of flying again?"

"No."

"Do you want to fly today?"

42

Peter thought for a moment. "I would rather not," he said. "But I should like to fly tomorrow."

"Hm," said Bjerke. "There is no reason why you should not. You have no injuries of any importance. But let us talk about that at breakfast tomorrow. You have had a very bad shake-up."

Major Tangen, the squadron leader, and Geir were sitting outside in a jeep waiting for him. They drove him to his quarters and stayed in his room while he changed his clothes.

"I have telephoned your parents," said Tangen, sitting down. "They would like you to ring them sometime. If you would like some leave you can certainly have it."

"No, thank you. Besides, the Crash Commission will want to question me, won't they?"

"Yes, but you can take some leave afterwards if you wish."

"I don't want any leave."

"You'll lose nothing by it. It will be some time before you can fly again."

Peter stood there with his shirt round his neck and one arm half-way into a sleeve. He looked at Geir as if seeking for help, but Geir was standing at the window with his back to him.

"What I need is to fly again," said Peter quietly. "There's nothing wrong with me, Dr. Bjerke said . . ."

Major Tangen rose, and stood jangling a bunch of keys in his pocket. "He certainly did not say that you *ought* to fly," he interrupted Peter. "I have spoken to the Commanding Officer, and we agree that you should be grounded for the time being."

Geir turned round.

Peter looked from one to the other, his mouth open. He was on the point of saying something, but shut his mouth with a snap and pulled on his shirt with impatient, abrupt movements.

"See you in the mess," said Tangen, and went towards the door. He stood there with his hand on the latch, waiting a moment, but no one spoke again. He nodded and left them.

As soon as the door was shut Peter began raging round, and chucking his flying clothes and boots into his locker. He kicked the door so violently that it almost flew off its hinges.

"Keep calm," said Geir. "Is there any reason why you should be upset? You might have had something a good deal worse than a temporary grounding."

"Of course, I know that. But what have I done wrong? Was there anything wrong with my flying?"

"No one has said that."

"Not directly, no. But that may well be the underlying reason. Why, I can't imagine. It wasn't my fault that the oxygen system failed, nor that I was obliged to let the plane crash. I cannot see any reason for stopping me flying. What about that ski-jumper you once mentioned?"

Geir shrugged his shoulders impatiently.

"If he had injured himself he would have kept away from the ski-jump for some time. Surely that is obvious."

"Have I injured myself, then?"

"Not physically, but your nerves have been under a very heavy strain."

Peter flushed, and took a step nearer.

"Say it," he shouted suddenly, throwing his arms about, "Say it straight out! You think I shrieked because I was stiff with fright. You don't think I did anything to save myself before you gave me the order to bale out. You think that I did nothing, but that it was *you* who saved me."

Geir's square face changed in expression without moving

a muscle. The glance from under the dark eyebrows was icy cold.

"Sit down," he said.

He took time to light his pipe, and the room was quiet while he struck a match and puffed out some heavy clouds of smoke which rose towards the ceiling.

"Who told you that the scream was broadcast?" he asked.

"The helicopter pilot. I must have pushed the radio button when I pulled the stick."

Geir nodded.

"It almost frightened the wits out of us," he said. "Most probably it was a natural reaction after your faint. But, anyhow, it must be thoroughly investigated. It was *I* who suggested that you should be grounded until that had been done."

Peter looked down at the floor.

"Wouldn't it have been sufficient for me to have just a little leave?" he asked.

"Is there any difference?"

"Yes. No one would have thought *that* at all strange."

"Do you care so much about what others think?"

"Don't you?"

"Yes, indeed. But not when other considerations are so important that they must be put first. Honestly, Peter, do you feel any particular wish to fly again just now?"

"Yes," answered Peter shortly. And then he added: "If for nothing else, to show that I am not afraid of doing so."

Geir dropped his pipe on the floor. He picked it up again and twiddled the mouthpiece to make sure that it was not broken.

"You must really give in now. You don't mean that," he said. "You spoke about the ski-jumper a moment ago, but you don't understand at all. There is only one reason why he should jump again if he falls. He wants to convince *himself* that he can do it."

Peter supported his head on the palms of his hands.

"I know," he said in a tired voice. "But that doesn't help at all. Everybody will talk about it, and flying can never be quite the same again."

CHAPTER SIX

Before the Board

FROM midsummer onwards an almost tropical heat-wave spread over the whole of eastern Norway. The cockpits of the aircraft were like hothouses, and the asphalt between the slabs of concrete on the aerodrome melted from the heat. For once the Sports Officer was spared sour looks and protests when he refilled the swimming-pool with ice-cold water once a week.

Captain Robertsen went to Kjeller airport on a short technical course. When he returned he brought with him two antique cannons which had lain there for a century or more. They were driven to the hangar, rubbed up, and put in order. The mechanics gave them fuses and made round wooden plugs which fitted the bores. When they were tested the whole squadron came to watch. Robertsen put the fuses in place, pushed half a pound of gunpowder into each bore, and hammered in a wooden prop with a sledge-hammer. Then he lit the fuse, and there was a bang heard miles away. The wooden props were shattered and turned into fine wood dust.

After a final polishing-up and three coats of paint the cannons were christened George and Thomas, and placed at the bottom of the steps outside the dispersal hut. There they stood as an ornament until, at the beginning of July, the first squadron salute was fired on the squadron's ninth birthday.

The day began with a morning parade which became memorable to all who took part in it. It was George's fault. After Major Tangen had finished his speech it was George's turn, and he entirely took the wind out of Thomas's sails —although it was Thomas who gave the best salute.

The squadron stood at attention as the solemn moment approached. Captain Robertsen lit a match, and applied it. The whistling sound from George's fuse drowned the noise of the flag slapping weakly against the flagstaff.

But Thomas had a miserable baptism of fire. His wooden prop leaked. So instead of exploding into dust with a violent bang, it stayed put in the bore, letting out gunpowder gas through a crack in the side. A perfect cataract, a tidal wave, of gas streamed forth, forcing its way out with a hissing, piping whine that had a striking likeness to a certain human sound, except that the pitch was much higher.

Pi-i-i-i-u-u-u-s-s-s!!

The stiff, upright ranks moved a little. Some shoulders shook, some knees creaked. The solemn faces trembled a little. Eyes swivelled to the side, and lips were pressed tightly together.

Then—BANG!! Thomas exploded with a frightful boom, as if he wanted to make up both for himself and for his brother.

Suddenly somebody giggled, whereat a gasping, penetrating howl arose from the rows of mechanics. In a moment all solemnity was broken, everybody, as one man, yelled and gasped and roared with laughter. No one heard the Major shout, "Stand at ease". Maybe, he himself was too far gone to give the command.

It took three minutes to disperse the parade. For the rest of the day for no reason whatever explosion-like sounds and giggles were heard wherever the men from 317 Squadron were to be found.

The only one who did not take part whole-heartedly in all this gaiety was Peter. The time of waiting had deprived him entirely of his sense of humour. His grounding went on and on. The Crash Commission had finished its inquiries, and Torbjørn, who had been a member, told Peter it was definitely proved that a fault in the oxygen system was the cause of the disaster. Peter himself could not be blamed for anything. He had done the right thing by saving himself.

But Peter knew well enough why they were waiting. It was because of his scream. He would probably have to go before the Pilot Investigation Board, and they would not dare to let him fly again before an explanation had been found as to why he shrieked—whether he was frightened; whether he had reason to be frightened; if there was enough reason—in short, whether he was fitted to be a jet pilot.

Whether he was fitted——

Peter hardly spoke to the other pilots now. He was given small jobs on the squadron, and got on with them. If he had anything to do in the briefing-room he preferred to go when everyone else was away flying. He felt as if he were an outsider. His companions seemed to him quite different. He thought they looked at him with uncertain glances, as if they had been talking about him when he was not there, and were afraid that he had heard what had been said.

It was as though he no longer belonged to them. He kept to himself, and was silent—waiting.

Not even Geir said anything about the investigation, although he was one of the permanent members of the Board, and was bound to know in advance. It was Torbjørn who gave it away in a conversation which almost made them enemies. Torbjørn could not agree that it was unnecessary and unfair to make Peter go before the Investigation Board. On the contrary, he thought it was only common sense.

"But why?" asked Peter.

"Say rather—why not?" Torbjørn replied. "The Board won't do you any harm. You seem to regard it as a sort of judgment seat. But you are not going to be judged; they are simply going to find out whether it is safe to allow you to fly again. Surely the chief person to be interested in that is yourself."

"I think I am the best judge of that."

"Do you think so? I don't."

"Oh—you know what I mean. Other people can judge my flying better than I can; I know that. But that is not in question now. It is my nerves they are worrying about, and I know those best myself."

"I am not so sure of that either."

"Indeed? Can you tell me who else can be sure? Have they anything to go on beyond what I tell them?"

Torbjørn did not answer at once. He pulled a packet of cigarettes out of his pocket.

"You will, of course, tell them all you know," he said, "and from that they will be more able to draw the right conclusions than you are."

He lit a cigarette and left it dangling in his mouth.

Peter was furious. Torbjørn could look at it in this superior way because it was not he who had to come before the Board. He could not even imagine that anyone could doubt him. Torbjørn was safe both as far as his nerves and his flying were concerned. He had nothing to fear.

But had he himself anything to fear? Could anyone prove that his nerve had given way—when he did not think so himself?

No, no one could prove it. But an examination before an Investigation Board would be a blot on his record that he would never be able to wipe out.

"Was it the Crash Commission that suggested the investigation?" he asked.

"No——" Torbjørn shook his head. "Not directly, at any rate. But we pointed out that you had twice reacted wrongly in a dangerous situation, or rather—once wrongly and once late."

"Twice?"

"Yes—last spring, when you almost collided with Geir."

"Oh—yes. Of course. I am impressed. I see that you have done a very thorough bit of detective work. But have you also remembered that time when I fell down from a tree and sprained my ankle?"

"Don't be absurd. We do the best we can, as you would yourself if you were a member of a Commission."

"Very well. But I have a perfect right to disagree with your findings."

Torbjørn took the cigarette out of his mouth.

"Of course," he said; "we live in a free country. I should be only too glad to discuss it with you if you would stick to the point."

Peter fought to keep calm. A little later he half turned and said: "What's the good? If you have decided that I ought to have jumped before——"

"No, wait a moment," interrupted Torbjørn quickly. "Did I say that? I did not mean it. We only pointed out that it *might* have been possible."

"That makes a big difference."

"It certainly does. The decisive point is whether you jumped the very moment you became conscious. If you were conscious when you shrieked, you lost five precious seconds, which would have cost you your life if you had been a few thousand feet lower?"

Peter nodded thoughtfully. "And—the incident last spring?"

"That could be considered to have been just bad luck, if we were convinced you acted rightly now. If not, it is possible that both events had the same cause behind them—namely, that your nerve failed you in a difficult situation. That at any rate was what the Commission unanimously agreed."

"And that is what the Board want to find out, is it?"

"Yes."

"Do you think that there's anyone besides myself who can know when I became fully conscious again."

"The doctor at any rate can help you to find that out. It isn't certain that *you* know."

"Oh, indeed. Well, well, there are a great many things one does not know in this world."

Peter turned on his heel and went off without another word.

Still further days of waiting lay ahead of him. But one morning the waiting time came to an end. He was called before the Board and shown into the office of the station commander. The Board members were collected round the long table, and the station commander pointed to a chair at the bottom of it in a friendly way. He himself sat at the head of the table between Major Tangen and the doctor. Geir was there, as was to be expected, and also Torbjørn. The latter had been co-opted because he had been a member of the Crash Commission.

Peter sat down. The seat of his chair had been warmed by the sun shining straight on it through the window. This made him perspire immediately, and things went from bad to worse. His shirt clung to his body, and he longed to ask them to open a window, but did not dare to do so. Farther up the room a window behind the station commander was half open; in front of it the curtain bulged out like a sail and fell back again, bulged and fell back.

The examination began.

Peter suspected a trap in every question, and felt as if he

were an accused before a judge. The fact that the station commander opened the proceedings by telling him that they considered him one of their most promising pilots, and that there was nothing they wished more than to keep him with them, did not help. Neither did it help when the station commander assured him that no one wished to take him away from flying, unless it were necessary for his own safety. Nothing could help him if they stopped his flying. That to him would be an unfair sentence and a punishment.

The questions seemed to be unconnected and casual, so that it was a strain to remain on the watch the whole time. Sometimes he could not see what they were driving at, and that made him feel insecure. He involved himself in long explanations which he realised did not satisfy them. It grew warmer and warmer. The sun disappeared for a time, but reappeared in the next window. He sat in an uncomfortable position, and tried in vain to loosen his wet shirt from his body. It stuck everywhere. Runnels of sweat ran down from his knees, tickling his legs in an irritating way.

No one showed either by word or expression what he actually thought, and Peter was none the wiser when they had finished with him. He tumbled out on to the steps, and stood there in his wet shirt feeling the summer breeze like a cold blast. Three hours before he was to hear the result! Just after lunch—but he did not want any lunch.

He put one hand into his pocket and walked along, stooping. At the east end of the aerodrome he climbed over the locked gates and went along a path in the forest. The smell of the pine and juniper hit his nostrils. The forest grew denser, and it was half dark between the trees. The sun fell in slanting strips through the topmost branches, making round spots of light on the ground.

He walked faster and faster, following the path over a low hill to a little valley on the other side, at the bottom of which lay a tiny lake. He sat down on a stump and threw small pebbles into the water. There was no wind, and the rings from the stones widened out over the blank surface until they struck the shores.

He stayed there for the rest of the morning; when the stump felt hard he moved over to a piece of grass and lay with his arms under his head. The clouds sailed slowly across the sky. The aircraft began to come home for lunch, passing low over his head on their way to the aerodrome. The flies buzzed sleepily round him as he lay with dry, wide-open eyes following the clouds which passed in an endless line towards the north.

CHAPTER SEVEN

The Decision is Made

By the time the Board had reached the stage where the station commander was able to sum up what they had agreed upon, all the members had thrown off their coats and were sitting in their shirt-sleeves. A clerk was called in to write up the report.

"Let us go through what we know point by point," said the station commander. "To begin with—2nd Lieutenant Hovden is a promising pilot, well above the average. He has never shewn any fear of flying, and has never tried to avoid difficult exercises. He acts quickly and correctly during ordinary flights. We only know for sure that he made a mistake once—last spring, when he placed himself and his flight commander in danger of collision. That time it was considered as a chance misfortune. The crash that happened a few weeks ago was due to lack of oxygen. During the downward glide he regained consciousness at about 8,000 feet and tried to straighten out the plane. He cannot remember it himself, but a scream of terror was heard over the radio, and we imagine that he pressed the radio button inadvertently when he gripped the stick with both hands. The shriek itself is of no importance. Any of us, perhaps all of us, might be deadly frightened in a similar situation, but we are bound to demand that a pilot should act correctly even if he is frightened. 2nd Lieutenant Hovden did not do so until four or five seconds later. Only in the last possible moment did he do the correct thing—namely, bale out."

The station commander sat thinking for a few moments, then he bent forward with his elbows on the table, and pushed his fingers through his hair. He went on:

"The question is now whether he was fully conscious when he tried to straighten out the plane from its downward plunge. If we think so, it must mean that he lost his nerve, and we shall also have to consider that he did so last spring. But if we think that he was not fully conscious before the moment he jumped, there is nothing in the crash with which we can find fault, and we can continue to consider the episode last spring as a chance misfortune."

The station commander looked round in a questioning way. "It is either or," he finished. "If his nerve gave way, he must never sit in a plane again; if it did not fail him, he can fly tomorrow."

"Let's have another window open," groaned the doctor.

"Perhaps it might be an idea to stretch our legs a little," said the station commander.

They all agreed, and went over to stand by the open windows looking out over the aerodrome. Very little was said. Each one was trying to make up his mind.

When they returned to the table, Major Tangen said to the doctor, "Is it likely that a pilot who generally makes fewer mistakes than most, and who knows that the smallest mistake will endanger his life—is it likely that he will lose his head at the very moment he gets into real danger?"

"It is not impossible," said the doctor. "There are many ways of meeting danger. Some act in a cold, calculating manner, some instinctively, some excitedly, some blindly—and some do nothing at all but go stiff with fright. But I think a man who was not up to standard would have already betrayed himself in other and less dangerous situations."

56

"That is one point in favour of allowing him to fly, then?" said Tangen.

"Yes, I think so—and here is one more. Consciousness never comes back suddenly after lack of oxygen; the half-conscious state may last for quite a long time."

Torbjørn had scarcely said a word since the beginning. He had sat there listening with his head in one hand looking as if he were half asleep. His face was motionless. Only his eyes glided quickly from one to the other.

Suddenly he sat up straight in his chair and said: "I have made up my mind. I suggest that he should be allowed to continue flying."

"Why?" asked the station commander.

"Oh, there are many reasons," answered Torbjørn. "I know him well, and I know what he is good for in tricky situations. Besides, I heard the scream, and I cannot bring myself to believe that he would shriek like that if he were fully conscious. I also think that if he had been conscious at seven thousand to eight thousand feet he would have known that the situation was not as frightening as the scream tells us that he thought it was."

They all chewed on this—for some time.

"I agree," said Geir. "I vote that he should go on flying. My reasons are more or less the same."

"Is there anyone against that?" asked the station commander.

No one answered. "Shall we take it as decided, then?" he asked again.

They all nodded.

The station commander seized the telephone. "Bring in five cups of strong black coffee," he said. He put the receiver back and rubbed his hands together contentedly.

When Peter knocked at the door at one o'clock he was so nervous that his legs were trembling beneath him, but one glance round the room was enough. He knew the result instantly. The smiling, relieved faces round the table told him as plainly as did the words that followed that his time of trial was over. He listened intently when the findings were read, but his thoughts were elsewhere. When he came out on to the steps again he did not remember much of what he had heard, but he felt like a new man. He looked critically at a plane which was about to land. He had not done this for many a long day. The landing was *not* perfect.

He walked towards the mess, and felt intensely hungry. On his way he passed one of the repairing hangars and saw that a 317 plane was parked outside. Following an impulse, he flung himself up on to the platform.

A mechanic came quickly out through the hangar door when he saw Peter climbing into the cockpit, but when he came nearer and recognised him, he stood there watching for a moment and then went away again.

Peter opened the hood and climbed in; it was close and warm in there. The sun had baked the perspex for a long time.

The cockpit seemed a little strange to him. He put his feet on the pedals and gripped the stick. His eyes glanced over the instrument panel. He caught hold of the controls—the stick, throttle, mixture control, flaps. He went through the cockpit checks, murmured them over to himself, shut the canopy, touched the controls and switches again, and looked at each instrument in turn.

He flew in imagination. He started, rolled out, checked for take-off, pressed the throttle, was in the air, circled, checked for landing and landed.

Once more!

It became too hot with the canopy lowered. He opened it and drew a deep breath, but did not feel quite happy about himself. He ought to have been able to do all this with his eyes shut—almost without thinking. His grip on the controls ought to have been surer, his eye quicker, his thoughts more alert.

He leant backwards in his seat and shut his eyes. Flew. He pushed the throttle fully forward, pulled the stick, imagined the needles trembling between the red strokes, the stick vibrating against the palm of his hand.

He opened his eyes; the instrument panel was dead, without movement, without life.

It was this that was missing. He would of course be in contact with the plane again as soon as it had life in it.

"Hi—are you going in for dry training?" Torbjørn approached him, cycling from the group headquarters. He

59

came up to the side of the plane and remained sitting on his bicycle, leaning one hand against the tip of a wing.

Peter did not answer; he just nodded.

"You're satisfied now, aren't you?" said Torbjørn, looking pleased.

The answer came to Peter from somewhere or other, he did not know where. He seemed to snap it up and throw it out as if it were not his.

"Are *you*?"

CHAPTER EIGHT

In the Air Again

HIGH heaven. Not a cloud. Not a breath of wind.

Peter jumped out of the jeep and remained on the platform as the others disappeared into the dispersal hut. The planes had been taken out of the hangars and stood in lines along the tarmac. His own was, as usual, between Geir's and Torbjørn's. One of the mechanics stood on the ladder attending to something in the cockpit. He looked up, smiling.

"Is it ready?" asked Peter.

"Yes. Are you going up?"

"In an hour's time."

The mechanic nodded, rubbing his hands with cotton waste.

"It's in prime condition," he said. "We have looked after it very carefully. One of the new ones had it for a trip or two, but it was all right. We've got a good plane. No nonsense about it."

His voice was proud, for the plane was his as much as it was Peter's. Without his patient and conscientious care it could not fly. That was his pride, and Peter's best guarantee.

Peter went back to the dispersal hut, and opened his locker in the corridor. His helmet, his flying-clothes, his boots, and parachute all hung in their places. He shut his locker, opened the door of the briefing-room, and was met by the well-known sight of early morning confusion and disorder. The boys sat or half lay in the chairs, with their feet far out over the floor or their legs dangling over the arms. Cigarette smoke lay like a billowing veil in the air, chatter and laughter and gay shouts blended into a buzz of sounds.

Peter waited a moment just inside the door, looking round the room. Geir, Torbjørn, and Terje were all sitting together at a table. An empty chair stood there too, and Peter felt a little stab of gratitude. He was accepted. He belonged there again.

"Hi!" Terje had noticed him and waved.

At that moment the squadron commander came in, so that Peter was able to slip into his place without saying anything until the briefing on the day's exercises was over.

Afterwards he listened with half an ear while Geir went through the exercise that D-Wing was to fly—without him.

He was to fly alone. Freely and frankly. For once he was to be allowed to frolic as he pleased.

"Peter——!" Geir pointed at him with a pencil. "You are to take off a quarter of an hour after us," he said. "Keep in touch with flying control and go up into the Valdres district. There you will not be in anyone's way. Keep to 20,000 feet, and fly a limbering-up programme with a few aerobatics thrown in. Don't forget that four weeks away from flying is enough to put you off your stride. See that you have all the checks in your head, and be careful not to forget anything. Read through the cockpit checks before you go up."

"I remember them," said Peter lightly.

"I said—'read over the cockpit checks before you go up'."

Peter started. It was a long time since he had heard that sharp note in Geir's voice.

"Certainly," he said.

He fetched the handbook and sat down to read while the others went off to start up. A little later he went into the corridor and put on his flying-clothes.

The mechanics were waiting beside the aircraft. One of them helped him to fasten his parachute and his seat belt. The other prepared to plug in the battery, while Peter went through the cockpit check.

"Contact!"

Peter turned up his thumb; the mechanic standing in front with the fire extinguisher relayed the sign to the one who was waiting with the battery plug.

"Contact!" A nod. The current was on. Some of the instruments came to life.

Peter put his hand on the starter. His fingertips trembled a little. Click. The starter engine buzzed. The sound took on a thin undertone when the compressor began to move.

Needles oscillated and moved forward. He pressed the starter. The petrol pumps worked. A bang. The tail spat out flame. The aircraft pitched a little forward, the noise changed from a deep roar to a shrill whistle which rose evenly, and eventually developed an irritable, piercing, cutting tone.

Peter pushed the throttle forward, keeping an eye on the temperature and pressure indicators. Everything was normal. He listened for extraneous noises, but heard none. He was ready. A quick glance round. A sign to the mechanics to bend down under the wings and draw away the chocks. One of them indicated that all was clear and Peter released the parking brake. The aircraft moved forward.

He called the air traffic control as he taxied out, and received permission to proceed. No aircraft was to be seen either on the ground or in the air. He had a clear run. Temperature, revs., hydraulic pressure, fuel, oil pressure— his eyes passed systematically over the indicators, buttons, switches, and handles. He pressed the canopy button, and the roof slid down and locked.

"Gardermoen from Wildcat 61. May I take off? Over."

"Wildcat 61. You are cleared for take-off. Wind variable, zero to two knots. Over."

He quickly adjusted his helmet and half lowered the flaps. The plane moved reluctantly and heavily forward. The engine needed more air. Not until the speed pressed the air in large quantities through the gap in the nose could the engine burn enough fuel to sling the jet stream backwards with full strength. Speed created more speed. After a few hundred yards the intense whine grew sharper; Peter was pushed against the backrest of the seat. The liberated powers in the engine trembled through the fuselage and passed through the stick and his fingers to his body. The grass along the edges of the runway became grey and striped. The speedometer took a leap forward. The end of the runway came towards him. He threw a last look at the instrument panel, pulled the stick lightly, and was in the air.

Then he relaxed. Not until then did he realise how intensely he had concentrated during his take-off. Could four weeks mean so much? Was it uncertainty that had made him tense all his muscles? Was it not rather that there was a little doubt lurking at the back of his mind?

He pulled up the wheels and the flaps. The ground sank quickly below him. At 15,000 feet, he regulated the air pressure in the cockpit and opened the oxygen valve. He kept his course straight towards the north-west.

In the clear air he could see far over the Hardanger plain. The shadows on the mountains were dark blue. The contours in the shadowed parts were almost washed out, but elsewhere they shone clearly, as if to compensate. The rivers lay like white bands on the terrain.

It was a lifeless landscape, a landscape without movement, like a highly-coloured map. Peter got the feeling that time was standing still. The water had gone stiff in the rivers; smoke rose in immovable columns from chimneys; trains and cars stood still. When he looked at the blue sky he felt that he himself hung motionless in space.

With a start he dragged himself away from his thoughts. He waggled the stick a little from side to side, and crisscrossed forward. By degrees he made his turns shorter and felt his way with two fingers on the stick. He tried a roll, and lost height. One more, with the nose higher. Then one more. He criss-crossed again, felt for the contact with the aircraft, and gave himself plenty of time. It was very quiet in the cockpit; the sound of the engine seemed far away and unreal, and the radio had been silent for a long time.

The movements with the stick became more abrupt. He went into a shallow dive of a few thousand feet. Then he

E

pulled up perpendicularly, went over on his back, and out into a half roll. Down again. A little steeper. Up again into two rolls and a loop on top. Down—more steeply, more quickly—perpendicularly—engine full out. His eyes flitted from ground to machmeter. The back of his seat pinched his backbone and he heard his own quick breathing within his rubber mask

A weak vibration shook the plane. He sat ready, closed the throttle, and pulled the stick evenly. The ground tilted and blue sky filled the front window again. Up—up. The machmeter and the altimeter whirled in opposite directions. The plane grew unsteady, the stick loose and fickle. The wings rocked. He kicked the pedal, and went into a spin with the ground showing like a whirling gramophone record in the front pane.

A red light—a warning light on the instrument panel. The front tank would soon be empty. He clicked over to the rear tank and the light went out. The spin was accelerating. It was time to straighten out. The rudder pedal right in, the stick neutral, engine full out. The gramophone record stopped whirling, and the plane came softly out of the spin.

Peter relaxed. He was sweating heavily. He had the aircraft in the hollow of his hand and felt that contact was re-established. He felt more strongly than ever before that flying was something he could never give up. It meant living every hour as intensely as if it were his last. It meant his own strength and power increased tenfold and at the same time stretched to breaking-point.

"I can't give it up," he thought swiftly. And later, wondering at himself! "But I haven't got to give it up!"

From far away came Geir's voice, filling the cockpit, asking Gardermoen for permission for Wildcat Blue to land. Peter looked at his watch. It was time to get home.

Suddenly he felt very lonely.

CHAPTER NINE

Nagging Doubts

"Look out! Look out! Look out!"

Peter stood shivering on the floor, staring into the darkness with wide-open eyes. His shout trembled like an echo in his ears, while an inexplicable fear ran like cold shivers up and down his spine.

He turned on the light. His pillows lay spread about the floor, and his pyjamas were sticking to his body, soaked in sweat.

He stood for a long time shivering, his eyes fixed on the dark window-pane. Then he pulled off his pyjamas, put on a clean pair, and got into bed again. But he left the light on.

He saw dawn approaching, and only dozed off now and then. But when he dozed he threw himself about restlessly, waking again and again.

One thought nagged at his mind: "Had anyone heard him?"

He was up long before reveillé sounded, and had finished breakfast before anyone else had come into the mess. He shirked the morning meeting, went straight to the squadron, and took half an hour to get there.

For once in a while it was raining—a drizzle from low, grey skies. August had come, and it might well be that the best part of the summer was over. Already the nights were cold and dark. By the time he put out the light the night was dead black, and in this deep darkness came those unpleasant

67

thoughts that kept him awake far into the small hours. There seemed a sort of magic in words, for the words he had said to Geir long ago, that flying would never be the same again after he had been grounded, had come true. He was back in his old place in the wing, he flew as well as he had ever flown, and probably most people had forgotten that he had once been grounded. But he himself could not forget it.

Yes, he forgot it when he was flying alone. He felt secure and happy as long as he was by himself, but in formation, with the others close around him, he became insecure and vacillating, and when Geir turned his head in the cockpit and looked at him he felt as if he were being pricked with needles. Why was Geir looking at him? What was he looking for? Was he keeping an eye on him? More than he did before the crash? More than on Torbjørn and Terje?

Peter drew his mackintosh closer round him and walked with quicker steps. The ground was sodden under his feet.

Grey skies, a grey landscape. It suited his frame of mind. Always a nagging doubt, a sword of Damocles over his head. One little mistake, one tiny little mistake—and new suspicions, new doubts, another Board. . . .

Someone was sure to have heard his nightmare cry, and talk had perhaps already got going at the breakfast table.

He hung his raincoat up in the corridor and changed into his flying-boots, since his shoes were soaked through. He went into the briefing-room, and sat aimlessly turning over the pages of a technical manual until the others arrived.

"Where have you been?" asked Geir. "I could scarcely believe my eyes when I saw that you had been down to breakfast before me."

"I woke early and could not get to sleep again."

"Anything the matter?"

"No. I played truant. I have no excuse."

Geir gave him a side-long glance.

"Don't fly if you don't feel up to it," he said. "We are only going to do some instrument let-downs. There's no need for you to come unless you want to."

"Why shouldn't I come?" Peter's voice was hard and impatient, and he half turned his head away. "There is nothing wrong with me. Of course I'll fly."

But he climbed into the cockpit with distaste.

Two and two the aircraft taxied down the runway and took the air in pairs, leaving two thin lines of smoke behind them. A few moments later they were in the clouds.

They were heavy, compact clouds. The dampness from them collected itself into small rivulets which ran down the perspex. Peter saw Geir's aircraft as no more than a shadow, and had to keep fairly close to his wing lest he should lose sight of him altogether.

At six thousand feet they emerged into sunlight and flew above a magic cloud landscape with white, ragged mountain tops and deep chasms. To the left the shadow of his plane followed Peter, surrounded by an encircling rainbow—a strange phenomenon that only airmen see. Straight in front rose the Gaustad peak, a dark, snow-flecked mountain visible through the cloud layers.

When Geir had been given the first bearing from Gardermoen they began the return journey. The voice of the officer giving the bearings came over the radio at regular intervals, setting a new course: "Steer zero five degrees. Over."— "Steer zero eight degrees. Over."

The air was very bumpy. The planes were thrown about in strong air currents, and they kept a good distance from one another as long as they were in the clear.

"Wildcat Blue from Gardermoen Beacon—you are right above me. Descend! Over!"

Towards the west again. The planes put out their dive brakes and glided evenly, without hurry, towards the clouds.

Peter listened absently to the monotonous routine exchange of words between Geir and the controller. In five minutes they would be below the clouds and would be preparing to land. He knew the passage through the clouds by heart and saw it mentally as a pattern on a map. He had flown it so often in good weather that he knew what the terrain below them looked like. When they turned towards the runway they would pass a moor that resembled the head of a giraffe. The track on the map went in an arch along the long neck and then straight through a pool of water the eye of the giraffe.

When they turned they got the sun in their eyes. The

white cloud-tips reflected the sun's rays in an intense blinding light, making the cockpit seem darker and darker as they approached the clouds.

Peter manoeuvred himself nearer to Geir's plane again. He saw Torbjørn and Terje flying close to each other on the other side. They were preparing for poor visibility, and perhaps they had good reason for it. One or two piles of clouds towered in front of them, and it might well be that they would have to keep closer together than when they went up.

Suddenly grey, flickering dusk. Cascades of rain beating against the windscreen. The plane shook and trembled in the violently eddying air currents. They had flown straight into a heavy rainstorm.

Peter threw himself forward in his shoulder-straps and glued his eyes against the perspex. Geir's plane was nothing but an indistinct blur rising and sinking in violent, abrupt plunges. It was impossible to see how far away he was. Peter could not judge whether he was slipping away from him or coming towards him. In fact, he could hardly see the tips of his own wings clearly. Suddenly a torrent of rain poured down the pane, wiping out everything. Probably it only lasted a moment or two, but to Peter it seemed an eternity. He had a panicky feeling that he was being pushed to the right, and drawn as if by a magnet towards Geir's plane. An irresistible urge to get to a safe distance forced him to push the stick to the left with a desperate wrench. In a consecutive movement he heeled the plane over and back again. Meanwhile the torrential rain had stopped and the perspex had cleared.

A glance to the right was enough. Geir had gone.

Quickly—over to the instruments! A thick wall of cloud surrounded the cockpit. His eyes passed systematically over the instrument panel. Course, gliding angle, speed. The throttle a little back, so that he might drop behind. The little finger on the radio button.

"Blue Leader from Blue 2. Lost you. Have dropped behind. Continuing descent. Over."

Geir's voice was a little more highly pitched than usual. "O.K., Blue 2. Join formation in the circuit. Blue Leader out."

He was alone. The controller's monotonous voice gave a new course, the last one. They would soon be down. The altimeter showed 1,500 feet. Peter's eyes searched in front of him through the wet windscreen.

There—he passed a rift in the stratum of clouds, and glimpsed a wet, gleaming road. Into cloud again. Little runnels on the pane. Flickering glimpses of light through the mist.

Suddenly it was clear again. The runway appeared beneath him, black, damp with pools of water. Half a mile away and a little lower he saw the rest of D-Flight, preparing to land.

Peter cut short the turn and got into place in the formation on the crosswind leg.

When they swung in to the parking place and turned off the engines the mechanics came across the tarmac in oilskins. The rain drummed weakly on the perspex. Peter opened the canopy and pulled off his helmet. He leant his head against the back of his seat and let the cooling drops splash on to his face.

One of the mechanics put the ladder in place and climbed up it.

"A good trip?" he asked.

Peter looked at him. A few seconds' pause. Then he nodded.

"Splendid!" he said.

He got up, a bit stiff, and crawled out of the plane.

CHAPTER TEN

A Difficult Choice

ONE day he went to Dr. Bjerke.

"I've come to be psychoanalysed," he said with a shy smile.

"We'll see about that," said Bjerke. "What's wrong?"

"My nerves, I suppose. I'm frightened."

"Frightened to fly?"

"No—of making a mistake."

"Oh! Doesn't that add up to the same thing more or less?"

"Not altogether. In a way, perhaps. But only if it is the consequences you are thinking of—whether it's dangerous, and things of that sort. That is not what I am afraid of. It is the actual mistake that I fear." He tried to find a clear explanation. "I can't bear the thought that those who stand there waiting for the mistake to come shall have reason to say: 'There you are—wasn't that just what we feared?'"

"Who is waiting for you to make a mistake?"

"Everybody—it's only natural. Everyone wonders whether it was right to let me fly again."

"Indeed——?"

Dr. Bjerke pointed to a chair and rang for coffee. The corporal who brought it recognised Peter, nodded to him in a friendly way, and poured out coffee for them both. Bjerke sat down at his desk, put two lumps of sugar into his cup, and stirred it thoughtfully.

73

"As a matter of fact I have been meaning to have a chat with you," he said when the corporal had gone. "I heard a rumour that you had a nightmare the other night."

Peter started.

"Are they talking about that?" he asked.

"Oh yes, a little. At least two or three heard it, and you could not expect them to keep quiet." Bjerke blew the steam from his coffee and gulped down a mouthful. "Would you like to go on leave for a while?"

"Perhaps, unless it would be best to give up flying altogether."

Bjerke raised his eyebrows.

"That I could never believe," he said, looking down at his coffee cup. "Are you flying worse than before?"

"Rather the opposite."

"What sort of mistake are you actually afraid of making?"

Peter searched for an answer. "That would be a long story," he said at last.

"Out with it, then."

They finished their coffee, and Peter drew up his chair nearer the desk. He rested his elbows on his knees.

"Well"—he hesitated a little—"well, it began with my grounding, the Investigation Board, and all the upset about the crash. I expect you noticed that I was furious over it all and thought it was unfair and brutal."

He laughed ironically.

"I thought everyone wanted to get at me, and I defended myself tooth and nail."

He grew serious again, carefully smoothing out a crease in his trousers. Then he went on:

"I fully realise now that it was absurd of me to feel like that. They were all pleased to get me back to the Squadron

74

again, and I am sure no one wanted me to give up flying, unless there was real danger in it—for myself, I mean. I know that now. It was when I realised *that* that I began to be afraid."

Bjerke's face was quite expressionless. He flipped a paper-knife between his fingers and waited for Peter to continue. But when nothing more came he asked: "What were you really afraid of?"

"Of disappointing them; of disappointing you all. You decided that I would manage as well as anybody else in a difficult situation, didn't you? Well, if I did not, I should be letting you down with a bang!"

"Hm——"

"And that is not all. I led you up the garden path. All I said to the Board had only one object in view. Please note this: I was trying all along to prove that there was no ground for your suspicions. I was not trying to help you to find a correct solution. No, I tried all I could to hinder it. There was only one person who knew the matter inside out, and that was myself."

"If *anyone* knows," said Dr. Bjerke. "Even you cannot know for sure why you reacted as you did, and whether it was correct."

"No. But in flying one has to be sure that one's reactions are correct. When I came before the Board, I made it appear as if I were sure. You remember that? But it was not true."

"All right. But do you really and truly believe that you are unable to think quickly enough in a decisive moment?"

Peter shrugged his shoulders.

"I don't know! But I suppose the mere fact that I am not sure of it is enough. It makes me feel insecure. That in itself is dangerous. A few days ago I dropped out of formation in

the clouds. I lost sight of the flight commander, broke away, and chose the easiest way out. I just followed at a safe distance."

"But, surely, that was the correct thing to do?"

"Yes, yes, absolutely correct. It was not wrong in any way. It was the safest thing to do. But I could have managed with less of a break—without losing contact."

Bjerke tried to balance the paper-knife on his first finger, could not find the balancing point, and let it fall to the floor. He pushed it towards himself with his foot, picked it up, and tried again. "No one has blamed you in any way, have they?" he asked.

"No indeed. But surely you can understand that I can't

go on flying if I am constantly afraid of tangling myself up in something I can't pull off?"

"Yes, I understand that. I understand perfectly. Is it a collision you dread most?"

"Collision? Everybody's afraid of a collision. That's obvious. I'm not more afraid of collision than anyone else. There's not a man who is not deadly frightened of it. No, listen to this. Listen! Imagine that you are just on the point of collision. Here he is—here you are! Your wings are quite close to each other, and then his engine suddenly cuts out. Either you do something or—bang. That is a situation for which you must be prepared, but must not be nervous about. If you are sure of yourself, you will have no fear of such a situation. You are absolutely certain that, at the very moment that his wing approaches yours, you will pull the stick and glide either above or below him. But it's just of that I am no longer sure."

"Hm. More coffee?"

"No, thank you."

Dr. Bjerke rose and walked up and down with his hands in his pockets. He stopped at the window and remained there looking out.

"No one can be quite, quite sure how he will react in a dangerous situation," he said without turning round.

"Quite, quite sure? Well, there are some who have proved that they are all right."

"True enough. But, on the other hand, how many have never been tested?"

"I look at it in this way. Anyone who has been put to the test must think the matter over. If he is uncertain as to whether he has stood the test, he must take the consequences."

"Hm." That gave the doctor something to think about. He had indeed a hard nut to crack. He might as easily make

77

a mistake as Peter. But he was almost certain that Peter's difficulties were figments of the imagination, and that he had reached them through brooding.

"I don't think I dare psychoanalyse you," he said at length.

"You promised to try."

They both laughed.

Dr. Bjerke sat down again. He looked first at Peter, then out of the window, then back again at Peter. The paper-knife flipped up and down.

"You brood too much," he said. "I cannot see that there is anything at all wrong with you. But of one thing I'm dead certain—there soon will be, if you go on like this. What you actually said at the Board did not matter very much. We were judging you as a pilot, we imagined ourselves in the situation in which you had been, and were quite satisfied that you could not be blamed for anything at all." He noticed the sidelong glance with which Peter favoured him at this point. "We shall think the same even if you have another accident. An accident can happen to anyone."

"Were you all agreed, all of you?"

"Yes. It did not take long. We skirted the fringe of the subject for some time; we were as cautious as cats. But 2nd Lieutenant—what's the man's name now?"

"Nygård? Torbjørn Nygård?"

"That's it. He said he could not think of a single sensible reason for grounding you. Everyone agreed at once, and the whole thing was passed and finished within a few minutes."

"Oh, I see! Did Torbjørn really say that?" Peter chewed on that piece of information for some time. "Did he really? Are you trying to tell me that I am making a mountain out of a molehill?"

"I think the whole thing is simply an invention of your

brain, yes. But if you go on moping and brooding you will make yourself so nervous that you will have to give up flying, and with my blessing too!"

Two aircraft rolled past on the taxi strip a little way off. Both men followed them with their eyes until they disappeared in the direction of 317's hangar. Peter looked at his watch.

"I'll think about what you have said for a few weeks," he said. "But I haven't great hopes of getting it straightened out."

"Well, take the time you need and then come and talk to me again. Have you any objection to my speaking to your squadron commander about this?"

"Yes!"

"May I mention it to your flight commander, then?"

"No—I'd rather you didn't."

"I think you should say yes. Lieutenant Grand might well be able to help you. He is a very sound man, and you are great friends, I believe."

"Yes, we are, but I do not think that would make any difference. Geir—Lieutenant Grand—regards the service, especially flying, as something far above personal feelings."

"That is just the reason why I suggested him, just the reason why he might be the right person to help you. You are not asking for a friendly action; what you need is help to estimate the matter correctly."

"All right. If he can help *you* to estimate it correctly, go ahead. But *I* want to work it out for myself. I don't want to discuss it with him either as a friend or as my superior officer. Please tell him so!"

"All right," said Bjerke, rising. "As a matter of fact, I can give you one piece of advice straight away."

"Yes?"

79

"It would be a good idea to change your surroundings. Get yourself moved to another squadron."

Peter's mouth fell open.

"Another squad . . ."

He sat there gaping, entirely aghast. Then he rose and prepared to go.

"Not on your life," he burst out. "If I can't fly here, I won't fly at all."

CHAPTER ELEVEN

Escape

EARLY one morning a motley crowd assembled in the brief-ing-room at Gardermoen. They were the pilots who were taking part in the yearly "Operation Escape", which was arranged to give the airmen some idea of how they should act if they suddenly found themselves escaping through enemy territory. All the men were in uniform, more or less cleverly disguised beneath civilian clothes, so that it would be quite difficult to determine whether they were airmen or not. Most of them had pullovers or wind-proof jackets over their battle-dress; some had an ordinary civilian coat and a sports cap; some had sports stockings up to the knee, mak-ing their trousers look almost like plus fours. But everyone was obliged to have part of his uniform showing, so that "the enemy" might be able to distinguish them from any other youngsters.

The escape exercise began somewhere in the neigh-bourhood of Kongsvinger and ended at Rygge aerodrome. That meant nearly 200 miles to be covered in three days and nights exactly—neither more nor less. Civil Defence, the police, and all railway officials of whatever grade, were "enemies", and it had been stated in the papers that anyone who felt so inclined might help the enemy in the chase. Generally, only about a quarter of the escapees managed to get through safely.

Svein was among those who came from Rygge. He took

it as a foregone conclusion that Geir and Peter would let him join them, and to this, of course, they both agreed. They all three sat together in the front row when the leader of the exercise went through it with them. Svein had a black pullover over his battle-dress and looked like a heavy-weight boxer on a training course. Geir and Peter wore wind-jackets.

"The worst of it is that we shall die of starvation before the first day is out," whispered Svein. The little box containing the emergency rations almost disappeared within his huge fist.

"This portion is supposed to last for twenty-four hours," Geir whispered back.

Svein looked at the little box, and turned up his eyes until

the whites showed. "It's not enough for a lunch," he groaned.

"I expect we'll manage."

"Without money—and enemies everywhere?"

"Oh, I expect we shall find some friendly soul. Some decent girl or something of that sort."

Svein brightened. "Yes, if we are invited to a meal anywhere we'll just stay there until the exercise is over," he whispered. "There must be limits to the dangers to which we are to be exposed."

They were each handed a map. The officer in command impressed on them that the exercise must be carried out by lawful means, and that they must not pay either for food or for a lift, either with cash or by credit. The only illegal thing they were allowed to do was to board a train and stay on it without paying if they could. The railways had agreed to this.

They were loaded into buses and driven to an isolated spot in the forest round Kongsvinger. By ten o'clock they had all been thrust out of the buses; a hundred men released all at once. There were airmen everywhere; the fields and the roads were peppered with them. A moment later they had all disappeared. The forest had swallowed them up.

Geir, Svein, and Peter ran through a bog, the water and mud splashing up around them.

"We must get as far as we can into the forest before the hunt begins," panted Geir.

"No. Wait a bit. We must make a plan. We shan't find food in the forest," shouted Svein.

"Yes, we shall; I *have* made a plan. I have fishing lines with me."

They had reached firm ground on the other side of the bog, and stopped for a moment to get their breath.

"If Peter agrees, I suggest we make you the planner, the fisherman, and the leader of the expedition," Svein said to Geir.

"That's O.K. by me," said Peter.

Geir sat down on a tree stump and spread out the map.

"In an hour's time we shall arrive at this lake," he said, pointing. "No one will look for us as far in the forest as that. So we can take things calmly until the Civil Defence people have got over their first fervour and have simmered down a bit."

It was a good suggestion, and, as neither of the other two had anything against it, they walked on. The sun burnt their necks; their boots were sodden with bog water and squelched with each step they took. When they reached the lake the sun was almost at its height, and the air above the forest quivered with heat.

They had a refreshing swim in the lake, and sunbathed for a while before they pulled on their trousers, hanging the rest of their clothes on branches. Geir selected and cut a pliable branch from a rowan tree, and Peter dug for worms, while Svein collected stones for a fireplace.

When Geir had fixed his line on his improvised fishing-rod they all three waited expectantly for a bite.

"I thought," said Geir, "that it would be a good plan to stay here quietly the whole day. There's no hurry. At this very moment the hunt for us is at its height. If we wait, and in that way get right at the back of the queue, the enemy will think that everyone has passed, and we shall get through more easily and quickly."

"Agreed," said Svein, "but only if we get fish."

They got fish—fine trout which they grilled on the embers as soon as they had pulled them out of the water. Even Svein had to agree that they were not in danger of starvation.

In the evening they collected pine-needles and made themselves beds. It was rather cold during the night, and they were sometimes obliged to get up and move about to keep warm. But by four o'clock the sun had risen, and they slept well for the rest of the night. Not until late in the morning did they take their bearings by the sun and their watches, and set off for Sander railway station.

Not an enemy to be seen until, late in the afternoon, the station came into sight several fields away. The station-master was the first man they saw. He was standing on the platform, looking this way and that as if expecting a train.

A by-way across the fields and through a little grove brought them to the railway line just over a mile east of the station. From there they followed the ditches down the line, sneaking along like thieves in the night. In the outskirts of the station surroundings they found a hiding-place behind a pile of planks, and waited.

Time passed. Svein was starving and they were just about to open one of their ration boxes when they heard that singing on the lines which heralds an approaching train. In a very short time it drew up at the station. It was a goods train. The last truck stopped about thirty yards from them. It was an open goods-truck with high sides.

"That's First Class, I'm sure," said Svein. "We'll take that one."

Geir peered down the platform. A few railwaymen were unloading cases from one of the front wagons, but it did not look as if there was anything to be done at the back of the train. Here was their chance. They could at least try.

"All clear! Go!" whispered Geir.

A moment later they all lay panting, hidden below the high sides of the truck. Almost immediately the train began to move.

But they were impossibly uncomfortable. The van was

full of cases. The train rocked, jolted, and rattled along, and so did the goods. They were obliged to sit up, so that their heads and the upper part of their bodies were visible to anyone who cared to look. But by degrees they realised that no one was interested either in the train or in them. After that they enjoyed themselves sitting in the sun. Svein opened a ration box and sighed: " 'Here is abundance', said the fly as he lay drowning in the milk jug!"

At the stations, each took it in turn to keep watch with his head above the sides of the truck. Geir had obviously been right when he said that it was safest to stay at the back of the queue. The station officials were not suspicious. The previous day every train had been carefully watched and searched, but now no one expected to find anything. Had the Civil Defence people been a little less vigilant as well, they might have had a very quiet trip to Oslo.

But just before they reached Aarnes Station, Svein suddenly gave a shout and pointed to three Civil Defence men running at full speed along the road. "I scent danger!" he said.

"Sure!" said Geir. "They are on their way to the station to catch us. We must drop off in double-quick time as soon as we stop."

"Easier said than done!" said Peter.

And he was right. The train drew up far along the platform, which was crowded. There was no chance of getting away without being seen. They reckoned that it would take the Civil Defence people ten to fifteen minutes to reach the station, and decided to wait until the last possible moment, hoping that the train would move on before the pursuers arrived.

They kept their fingers crossed and waited. Heavy goods-train doors were banged open and shut. Five minutes passed —six—seven—eight. Geir stuck his head above the edge, and ducked down again quickly.

"They're coming," he said. "We've just two or three minutes in which to decide."

"There's no choice," contended Peter. "If we jump off now we shall be caught anyway."

"I promise you I'll never set a mousetrap again," declared Svein.

Geir looked out again.

At that very moment the station-master blew his whistle. A long time—half a minute or so—passed before the wheels began to turn. The train pulled slowly out of the station. Svein lifted a hand over the high side and waved.

But the situation was not saved, not by a long way. Obviously, the railway officials would telephone to the next station, and arrange for a receiving committee to meet and greet them there as soon as the train arrived.

"We must jump off," said Svein.

"You're crazy," cried Peter.

Geir thought hard. "We must change wagons," he stated.

"Isn't this comfortable enough?" asked Svein.

"Yes, indeed it is. But it is for this truck the reception will be prepared. Unless I am mistaken, they will all stand at the end of the platform waiting—the station-master and the whole lot of them; both those who are there by rights and those who are purely curious. When the train stops they will all stare at this one truck. Then we will jump out of another, and shall at any rate have a start!"

"Fine," answered Svein. "Come on!"

They crept from truck to truck, helping each other. As the train consisted entirely of open trucks, the escapees got almost as far as the engine. They had a feeling that they were overstepping the mark as to what was allowed. But that could not be helped, for there was no other way out. When they reached the next stop they said goodbye to caution, clambered down on to the platform, and, with their

87

hands in their pockets, sauntered nonchalantly out of the station. No one stopped them, but there were at least ten men collected round the end truck.

As soon as they were clear of the station, they took to their heels and disappeared into the first clump of trees they could see. From there they followed a sort of depression in the ground until they approached the main road again, a few miles to the south.

"Now we must find a telephone box and call the railway station," said Geir. "Otherwise they are sure to think we have jumped off, and will send out a rescue squad to pick up our remains."

"You wait here," said Peter. "I'll fix it."

Before they could stop him he was on the main road, walking in the direction of the nearest farm, in full view of anyone who might be looking.

"Surely it was not necessary for him to be quite so imprudent," murmured Svein.

"No——" Geir lay down on his back in the heather, and lit his pipe. "But this exercise doesn't interest him enough to matter to him." He took off the mouthpiece of his pipe and blew it clear. "Peter has changed a good deal lately, Svein."

Svein scratched the back of his neck. "He looks punctured," he said, "as if all the spirit had gone out of him. Was it the Board that did that to him?"

Geir blew smoke rings. "Yes, first of all. But I'm afraid he is brooding about worse things than that."

"What?"

"He's thinking of giving up flying." Geir followed a smoke-ring with his eyes. The faint breeze drove it into the air, and tore it into ribbons. "Dr. Bjerke told me that he went to him for advice. Bjerke hoped I might find some way of helping him; but it isn't so easy, because Peter won't talk things out."

88

"Hm. . . . What sort of an idea has he got into his head?"

"Oh, you know the sort of thing. Peter is not as tough as you, or me, for that matter. An affair of that sort might perhaps have made us fly better than ever. I imagine that we would have thought we'd show them that we—and the Board—were right. But *he* wonders whether the Board was right."

"Good gracious me!" muttered Svein. "But we ought to be able to talk him back to sense."

Geir shook his head. "I don't believe we can," he said. "He will need more than talk. He will need proof, if it's to be any good. I am afraid that's the only thing he'll acknowledge."

"Bad job!" answered Svein.

CHAPTER TWELVE

Towards the Goal

SVEIN hummed contentedly as he settled himself down between sacks and boxes. The three of them had been given a lift on a lorry which was going to Lilleström. Dusk was falling, and they shivered a little in the chilly evening air; but they reached Lilleström without being stopped, the police having withdrawn their guards for the night.

The driver was a good-natured man who thought it fun to help them. He took them home with him and put them up for the night, giving them both supper and breakfast; and in the morning he drove them through the town and part of the way on towards the south.

They began to walk along the main road. They were all bearded by now, and were soon pretty dirty after a few miles on the dusty road. They turned off into the forest when they saw people, and threw themselves down into roadside ditches when they heard cars coming. Now and again they glimpsed Civil Defence people on motor-cycles or in cars, and realised that they had come to a part of the country where the hounds were in full cry.

"Shall we have to *walk* all the way to Rygge?" asked Peter after some time.

"In that case I shall have to get hold of some sort of foot-plaster," answered Svein. His feet were already chafed and painful.

"As far as I'm concerned we might as well take our chance with a car now as later," said Geir.

Peter stopped. "Slip into the forest, then."

"It's not your turn to thumb one," protested Geir.

"Oh, go on!" Peter waved him on. "It doesn't matter who does it. You've got no more chance than a snowball in the Sahara with that unshaven face of yours. If we're going to get a lift I'd better do it, as I don't look quite as ghastly as either of you."

A private car approached them at full speed, so that there was no more time for further discussion. Geir and Svein plunged into the ditch at the roadside.

The brakes screeched, the car stopped.

"Hullo," said the man at the wheel. He saluted Peter cheerfully with his hand to the brim of his hat. "One of the runaways, I presume!"

"Yes!"

"Jump in. I'm a commercial traveller, and the back of the car is full of boxes and parcels. But there's plenty of room for you."

"There are three of us!"

"The more the merrier. That will be all right. Dig your-selves in. It will be fun to see whether we can fool any-body."

So they were on their way south again. They packed themselves into the back seat as best they could, and each of them held a box in his hand behind which to hide if they were stopped. But the car, a brand-new Ford, rushed gaily along until they had to slacken speed as they passed through Askim. There they were stopped by a police con-stable.

"Car-control?" asked the man who was driving.

"Not today. I'm looking for refugees. Did you see any-thing suspicious on the road?"

"No! Are they dangerous?"

"No, not particularly. They're airmen who are carrying out an exercise!"

"Of course! I read about it in the paper. Yes—I saw a couple of bearded men sitting at the wayside a few miles north from here."

"Thanks for the information," said the constable. He started up his motor-cycle and went off northwards.

A little south of Askim they had to get out, as their host was not going any farther. They settled themselves down among the trees in a little hollow, and held a council of war while they ate their remaining rations.

"We've plenty of time," remarked Geir. "It's only half-past twelve, and we haven't got to be in Rygge until eight o'clock tomorrow morning."

"We've certainly got time enough," replied Svein; "but we can't live on that until tomorrow morning. We must have food."

"Hi there!" cried Peter, jumping down on to the road. He was hailing a pretty girl about seventeen years old, who drew back, terrified at the grim-looking apparition.

"I am quite harmless," said Peter. "I'm only a poor air-man suffering from the rigours of camp life."

"Oh!" she relaxed and smiled. "I know all about you. My brother is in the Civil Defence, and he has been out looking for you."

"Aha," whispered Svein to Geir, "not too good!"

"Sssh!" said Geir.

"I won't give you away," said the girl to Peter.

"Thank you, but I don't mind if you report those two up there!" announced Peter, pointing to the two black faces lurking in the heather.

She laughed. "I won't report them either!"

"That one with the bleached hair and the huge eagle's nose is just about starving to death. Do you know any place where we could go to get some food?"

"I forgive him," whispered Svein.

The girl considered. "I'll ask mother," she answered. "Perhaps you can have dinner with us!"

"With him—your Civil Defence brother?"

She shook her golden curls. "He's a lorry-driver, and he's on a job today."

"Then I can say thanks a thousand. Shall I wait here?"

"You can come with me if you like," she said. "It's just round the corner over there."

Svein lay on a clump of heather with his chin resting on his hand. "He's not lost all his spunk, after all!" he said, rolling over on to his back. He crossed his arms behind his head, and chewed a piece of straw thoughtfully. "I wonder what we can do to help the lad!"

"I've thought of something," replied Geir. "I haven't only thought, I have decided to act—almost. But it's so off-track that I hardly like to talk about it."

"Oh. What seems off-track to you might be the middle of the road to us ordinary people. Don't worry!"

"No, I'm in earnest this time!"

"All the better. It's always good to see one's ideal stepping off the straight and narrow. It strengthens one's own self-esteem!"

Geir smiled, but the expression on his face did not correspond. He was half amused, half serious.

"It seems to me," he said hesitatingly, "that if Peter were in a really dangerous situation and cleared it correctly he would then have the proof he needs."

The straw fell out of Svein's mouth, and lay forming a bridge from his chin to his chest. He gazed at Geir with half-open mouth.

"You're crazy," he groaned, sitting upright.

Geir did not answer.

"Are you going to *create* such a situation?"

"I thought so!"

"And if things go wrong?"

"I know a method that is fool proof!"

"A hundred per cent?"

"Ninety-nine and a half."

"The half per cent is the chance that you must not take!"

"I know that!"

They looked at each other.

Svein lit a cigarette, and spat on the match before he threw it among the heather.

"Is it the only way in which you can convince him?" he asked after a while.

"Sure," said Geir.

"And how are you going to do it?"

"I've been flying some solo trips practising it," answered Geir, holding out his two hands to represent two planes flying side by side. "I fly straight forward. Suddenly I heel over to the left with the wings almost perpendicular—that is, in a sudden turn towards Peter. But at the same time I push the stick right forward and put on full right rudder. The elevators will act as rudder and force the nose to keep straight on, and the rudder will act as elevator and hold the nose up—at any rate for a short time. The aircraft will swerve forwards and obliquely downward, and a moment later I shall straighten out or let the aircraft go into a spin."

"How far away will Peter be?"

"Ten yards. He will get the shock of his life, and will think that I am going to cut straight across his course. Then we shall see what he does. I have no doubt whatever but that he will shoot straight up into the air like a rocket."

"But if he doesn't—and if you swerve even a fraction?"

"That I shall not do. I have tried it. I have been successful every time. I have done it just a few yards above the clouds to see whether I swerve. Never the least little bit . . ."

Svein thought over the matter for a long time.

"*Et tu Brute!*" he murmured. "I didn't expect you to go off the beaten track."

"Pah! I've had my little sideslips as a pilot—like everybody else!"

"You don't say! When?"

"The first year—particularly."

"Well, well, that is natural. We were up to a lot of nonsense in our youth. Later we've developed more sense, happily. This will be your last prank before old age sets in, I suppose?"

"Yes, I promise you."

"Well, best of luck. I'll keep my fingers crossed. When are you going to do this great deed?"

"The day after tomorrow, before he has time to make a decision."

"Let's think of something else," said Svein. "He ought to be back with our invitation cards by now!"

A few minutes later they heard a whistle from the road, and sprang up. Peter was standing at the corner beckoning to them, and they did not take long to obey his summons.

"You're welcome to a meal," said the man who met them at the door. "Wonder what that son of mine will say when he hears of it."

They ate until they could eat no more, and between their mouthfuls they recounted all their adventures. It was a merry meal, and they were given coffee and home-made cakes to finish up with.

"If only my son were not in the Civil Defence he could have driven you almost to Rygge," said their host. "He takes goods to Moss every morning."

"When is he due there?" asked Svein.

"Seven o'clock."

"That would have fitted in beautifully."

They stayed with this hospitable family until the evening, when they had to leave, as the son in the Civil Defence was expected home. But they did not go far, for Svein had a plan. They settled down among some trees on the other side of the road, and waited until they saw the lorry arrive and swing into the yard. It was loaded with sacks and boxes.

"There you are," whispered Svein. "At dawn we'll hide ourselves among the cargo, and let the Civil Defence drive us to Moss."

The plan was adopted. They shivered through the cold hours of the night. About four o'clock they settled themselves as comfortably as possible among the sacks and boxes in the lorry. An hour later they were off.

There were two men in the driver's cabin. The airmen heard them talking, but the lorry was too noisy to distinguish what was said. Otherwise, everything was calm and comfortable, and the speed could not have been better. If this succeeded, they would reach "home" at just about the right time.

Once they were stopped by other members of the Civil Defence Force.

"Have you seen anyone?" they were asked.

"No," answered the men in the lorry. "Have you?"

"Oh yes! We caught a lot of them last night. They're pretty thick round about here now."

"Well, we'll keep our eyes open," said the two men in the lorry as they started the engine again.

About half-past six the lorry stopped suddenly, brakes screaming. The three escapees clutched at the cargo to avoid being squeezed flat.

"Did you see them?" shouted one of the men in the cabin to someone outside.

"Yes. They rushed into the forest. Come on!"

Lorry doors banged, and there was a sound of boots disappearing at a gallop among the trees.

"Travellers to Rygge alight here!" chanted Svein. He struggled to his knees, and moved a box, weighing a couple of hundredweight, to one side. Then he climbed down, and taking a sack of sugar, placed it in the driver's seat. "Give them our love, and thank them for the lift," he said, patting the sack on its shoulders.

They ran into the forest on the east side, as the lorry men had gone to the west. When they reached a little hill Geir climbed a tree, and orientated himself by means of his map. He found that they had a good hour's walk in front of them.

"We must steal through the forest, and stop and listen every hundred yards or so," he announced. "There are lots of people out after us here, and the first to hear his adversary, wins. There's no need to hurry. For the last half-hour we have our safe conducts. Then we can run, if it's necessary from the point of view of time."

G

But there was no need. Just before eight o'clock they stepped out of the forest in company with about thirty other bearded and dirty men.

The C.O. received them and congratulated them. After a shave, a shave, and a change of clothes, they sat down to a breakfast table groaning with good things.

"Here I stay," remarked Svein. "When I've finished my breakfast I shall begin on lunch; and when I've finished lunch I shall have my tea; and when I've finished tea I'll start on dinner."

CHAPTER THIRTEEN

Ordeal by Fire

PETER's thoughts wandered—

He was gazing idly at the landscape beneath him, and was aware of Geir's aircraft as a shadow to the right in his field of vision. The air outside the cockpit was crystal clear, and the ground seemed nearer than the altimeter showed. The colours were unusually bright, and the shadows were sharply outlined in the flood of light from the sun.

But the altimeter showed 20,000 feet.

Geir also kept his eye on the altimeter! He was climbing in a steep spiral, and continued for several minutes before he levelled out into a straight course. He glanced over the gauges, switches, and handles. Carefully and methodically he made the last preparations to carry out the plan he had in mind.

The Lake of Mjøsa lay in front, like a thin line towards Lillehammer; Gjøvik slid under one wing and disappeared. The planes drew condensation trails in straight lines across the sky.

Peter tried to concentrate on his flying, but his eyes moved slowly and absent-mindedly between the instruments, the ground, and Geir's aircraft. His thoughts were on other things.

"Is this the last time I shall fly?"

He knew that he must soon make a final decision. There was no point in postponing it any longer. The question followed him about like a nightmare as soon as he got into the air. All he saw and all he thought about was connected with it in one way or another, and, because he was absent-minded and unobservant, his flying had become uncertain and erratic.

A little turn distracted his thoughts for a moment. He followed automatically as Geir's wing tilted. His own went down when Geir's went up. The shifting was parallel and almost simultaneous, as if one single thought and a single pressure on the stick steered both planes. It was never difficult to follow when Geir was leading. His manoeuvres were always gentle, with even, delicate transitions. Never a sudden unexpected movement. His plane was like a platform to hold on to.

It was just a trivial turn, one in a thousand, neither better nor worse than most. But Peter got the idea that he would remember it, in case this was the last time that he and Geir flew together.

A sucking feeling in his stomach, almost like hunger, bothered him. He turned the oxygen on full for a while, and took some deep breaths before he put the switch back to normal.

It stimulated him a little.

But the sucking feeling was still there. It was always there now when he was flying, a sort of grumbling that never stopped, even and continuous, impossible to get rid of.

He knew its origin. His nerves were on edge. He carried a terror picture within him. At any time something might happen quickly and without warning which would demand that he should think and act with lightning speed. Would he be able to respond? Perhaps. Perhaps not. It was terrifying to feel that he was not sure. His self-confidence had taken a nasty knock, and this consequent uneasiness was a danger in itself. It was wearing his nerves to bits the longer he went on with his flying.

Peter could easily imagine a catastrophe without feeling particularly afraid. An unavoidable catastrophe was a possibility with which every pilot had to reckon. But the thought that, if it happened, he might be paralysed by panic and unable to move a finger to help matters filled him with terror. Anything rather than that. Anything rather than the empty feeling of doing nothing when something *could* be done.

A white strip of smoke moved slowly southwards along the west side of the Mjøsa lake. A train on its way to Gjøvik. On their return he would look and see how far it had travelled. All trains looked the same from great heights—like thin white strips. In winter the smoke was grey.

Today, tomorrow, or the day after tomorrow, when he climbed out of the cockpit and met Geir on the tarmac, he would have to make up his mind. Probably he would say: "That was my last trip."

He knew that Geir's smile would stiffen. The firm, calm expression would disappear, and the persuasive arguments he would put forward would be stammering and uncertain. Neither Geir nor anyone else would dare to take the responsibility of persuading him to go on. There was too much at stake. Human life perhaps, both his own and his comrades'.

No, he must make the decision himself. No one could help him. He must make it himself—make it himself—make it himself.

Geir's voice on the radio broke into his thoughts, "Blue 2, pull away to fifteen—correction *ten*—yards' distance. Over."

"Ten yards. Out." Peter's answer was dry and matter-of-fact. He pulled the stick back and put himself into position.

Geir looked back quickly and measured the distance with

his eyes. Peter's aircraft seemed large and near, but the distance was right; it was the ten yards he had asked for.

Beads of perspiration stood out on his forehead. The cockpit felt oppressively hot, and his shirt clung to his back.

Was all clear? Was he clear? Had he planned carefully enough? Was he sure how he was going to do it? Had he foreseen all the dangers? Should he go over it once more?

There would be no point in that. The result would be the same. He could never rid himself of the doubt. On the contrary, the more he thought about it the more obvious it became that he ought to abandon the whole plan. For a long time he had wondered whether he should ask the squadron commander for permission. But he realised that the answer would most certainly be no. He must take the responsibility himself, the responsibility for all that might happen. There was no doubt about that. If Peter—— No, Peter would do the right thing. Peter would play his part, if he himself did his. He was sure of that.

He felt a pulse beating in his temples. He moved his feet to the top of the rudder pedals, and gripped the stick tighter.

Oh—come on——

With a hard push he slung the stick away from him, first to the left and then forwards—in a coherent movement, swift as lightning. The stick banged against its base. The right pedal down—the wings tilted violently to the perpendicular, and the jerk slung him brutally aside. His safety harness cut into his shoulder. . . .

Peter realised Geir's violent heel-over as something he both felt and saw. A start like an electric shock went through him. A swift reflection of the sun from Geir's wings came towards him like a projectile. *Towards* him! Good Lord—what was happening? Was Geir going to turn right across his nose? *Was he making straight for him?*

An impulse sprang from his brain which in a fraction of a second alerted every fibre in his body. Before he had time to complete the thought, he had pulled the stick as far back as it would go, and was squeezed down into his seat as by an intolerable weight. The centrifugal force drove the blood from his brain, and drew a blind in front of his eyes. It grew pitch dark. His helmet became as heavy as lead. His hold on the stick loosened, and his arms were pressed powerlessly against the floor.

He lay in a tight loop, which increased the weight of his body ten times.

With a sudden powerful effort he managed to shove the stick away from himself, relieving the pressure so much that he was able to lift his head and right himself. When his vision cleared, he lay on the top of the loop with his head down. He pressed the radio button and his breath came in a gasp: "Geir, what's the matter?"

But he got no response.

Geir heard him, but he was not able to answer. He could not even reach the radio button. The cockpit was chaos. He was no longer flying the plane, the plane was flying him.

Everything had developed in a mad rush and quite differently from what he had expected. One thing, one single thing he had forgotten. In the moment he flipped over towards Peter he had felt that he was not sitting well fastened in his seat, but that he was lifted up and slung against the cockpit walls. He had forgotten to tighten his shoulder-straps for aerobatic flying.

And then it happened——

He heard a crash. His helmet banged against the hood. He groaned and screwed up his eyes. For a short, confused moment he left the aircraft free. It took the power from him, and flipped suddenly over onto its back. When he felt that he was hanging in the straps he neutralised the stick and the pedals. But the nose had dug itself down, and he suddenly found himself in a steep inverted spin, a whirling spiral dive with the plane on its back.

The centrifugal force and the force of gravity threw him out of his seat, and pressed him together so that he hung like a bundle in his harness. His feet slipped off the pedals. His head was thrown back, and his forehead was thrust against the cockpit roof. He could scarcely reach the top end of the stick. His grip began to slip. His body swung rhythmically from side to side, dust and dirt from the floor whirled up and laid itself like sandpaper over his eyes. It was impossible to keep them open.

"Stretch out!" was the first panicking thought he had.

"Find the pedals. Get down on to the seat! Get down—get down!"

He stretched his body so that he stood in an arch between the shoulder-strap and the floor. His toes just reached the pedals. By stretching his shoulders almost out of joint, he was able to move his grip on the stick, and felt the radio button against his little finger.

Which way was he turning? He blinked his eyes, and tried to open them. In a quick glimpse he saw the ground above his head turning round and round, rolling like the deck of a ship in heavy seas. But these short glimpses were not enough to guide him. He could not tell which pedal he should use in order to stop the rotation.

His little finger shivered on the radio button. He was panting, and his voice shook. "Which way am I turning? Which way?"

"Left—use the right pedal!"

Peter answered at once, as if he had been waiting for the question. His voice sounded a little thinner than usual.

Geir turned to the side and stretched out his foot as far as he could reach. The pedal went in easily—too easily; it felt slack and ineffectual. There was scarcely any air resistance to the rudder. He held the stick as loosely as possible, so that it might find the neutral position of itself, but did not dare to let go his hold and risk not being able to find it again.

Seconds passed. Time was both endless and horribly short. Nothing happened. The spin continued at the same rate.

Should he shoot himself out? Sacrifice the aircraft?

Not yet! Not yet! He had got himself into this situation; it was all his own fault. What should he say afterwards? What should he say?

Something or other seemed to grip his throat. His

stomach contracted and new and unknown sensations went through marrow and bones. They sent a wave of icy feelings through his lumbar region. He felt like an animal in a trap. He had the choice between the aircraft and the parachute. He must think clearly, but he could not. He must reckon out the time, but did not know how many seconds he still had left. He must decide when he should jump, but decide rightly—not too soon, not too late. The one would cost him the aircraft, the other his life. He was in a race with time; as long as the aircraft could be saved he must stay where he was. But no longer.

Each second took him lower. The plane was whirling towards the ground without control, like a leaf in the wind. Once more he missed his hold on the pedals, losing precious seconds before he found them again. His thoughts were chaotic. Bale out; save the plane; bale out; save the plane.

Peter's voice broke into his whirling thoughts: "Can you manage?"

"No-o-o-o——"

All this time Peter had circled around Geir in steep spirals. He waited breathlessly for something to happen. He dared not mix himself up in it, and had no advice to give. He knew nothing more about inverted spins than what he had heard and read, and had been warned against. There was nothing he could do to help. He felt sure that Geir knew better than he did how to get out of a spin.

Geir's groaning breaths sounded in the earphones. His voice had a strange ring in it which Peter had never heard before. It was thin and helpless: "I—can't—get it out. How high—am I?"

"Fifteen thousand."

Peter shivered; his jaw was trembling as if he was chattering with cold. 14,000 feet. Geir's plane was going down quickly. Things were getting hot. Was there really nothing he could do to help? Was there nothing he could see that Geir could not see? Could there be anything wrong with the aircraft?

He looked at it. The rudders and the wings were undamaged. The drop-tanks hung in their place on the wings——

"The drop-tanks!" Peter gasped. The drop-tanks might be the cause. What if they were unevenly emptied? Would that put the plane out of balance, and involve it in steeper and steeper spirals?

He could not control his voice. In his excitement he shrieked at full strength into the microphone: "GEIR— RELEASE—THE DROP-TANKS."

Meanwhile Geir had been squeezed more and more together in his shoulder-straps, and hung so twisted that he could scarcely move. The muscles in his right leg were in process of knotting themselves into a stiff, painful lump. The blood was pressed against the back of his head, his temples, eardrums, and eyes. The air in the cockpit was a thick fog of dust, and his eyes were almost closed by dirt and tears. The world had shrunk into the little cockpit which hung upside down, endlessly turning round and round. A crazy world. A place where it was impossible to think a sensible thought. But into this shaking, trembling world came Peter's voice. It gave him a clear thought to take hold of. A new hope. The drop-tanks.

He hit out blindly for the release switch. The blow sent a shiver of pain up his arm, but he scarcely noticed it. He hit out once again and felt that the switch clicked over. It was done. The drop-tanks had gone, the wings were clear. The next few seconds would be decisive. This was his last chance. He held the right rudder tightly, and let go of the stick. It would find the neutral position automatically. If he did not get hold of it again it would not matter. He could do no more. If this were not successful the plane was lost. It would dig a deep hole in the ground, and explode into tiny bits of metal. He had wrecked it deliberately.

Was anything happening?

In but a few seconds he would have to make up his mind. But how long had he? What respite? How high was he? God in Heaven, how high was he?

He put his finger on the release mechanism. One second—two——

No. Wait a little longer! A little longer! Wait!

There must still be a respite.

Wasn't there a new rhythm in the tremors? Was the transition a little gentler? The pressure on his shoulders a little weaker? Was something happening? Was something happening at last?

It happened!

The rotation slowly died away. The aircraft came softly and willingly out of the spiral, and remained on its back in a steep dive. Half a roll and an even pull on the stick brought earth and sky into their right places. The seat received him, and he sank trembling down into it.

While he was still sitting there shaken and confused, rubbing the dust out of his eyes, he glimpsed a shadow in the corner of his eye, and saw that Peter had sailed up outside the side window. They exchanged a glance.

"Fine, Geir," said Peter warmly. And then in a louder tone of voice, "Are you all right!"

It was some time before Geir was able to answer. He was just about to do so when he was stopped by a shaken anxious voice asking urgently: "Wildcat Blue leader from Gardermoen. Is all under control?"

Geir looked round the cockpit. The dust had sunk back to the floor, leaving behind it a grey layer on all the ledges and handles. The instruments looked normal. No warning light was lit. And the aircraft hummed along evenly and calmly.

He cleared his throat and said "Ah-ah-ah" into the microphone as a test. He had a voice. He pressed the radio button, and answered Gardermoen in his usual measured monotonous tone: "Gardermoen from Blue leader. All under control. Position a little north of Gjövik. Height 8,000 feet. Course towards Gardermoen. Over."

The controller sounded relieved. "Blue leader—you are cleared for approach. Look out for helicopter north of Hurdal at about 3,000 feet. Over."

"O.K. Blue leader out."

They began a long, shallow descent.

Peter kept an eye on Geir for a time, but was reassured when he saw that all seemed normal.

Geir was sitting gazing calmly straight in front of him, and the aircraft was moving swiftly and steadily along. What had happened was to Peter an insoluble mystery. He was tempted to ask Geir how it began, but decided to wait until they were down. The reason for the sudden swerve was surely too involved to be explained in a few words over the radio. He felt that he must content himself with knowing that the danger was over.

He started. *The danger was over!* The thought struck him like a bomb. In his terror over what had happened to Geir he had scarcely realised that he himself also had been in danger. But he *had* been. In real danger. He had avoided a collision with Geir by a hand's breadth. He had reacted correctly. It was he—it was actually *he*—who had saved the situation.

As they flew downwards side by side he realised by degrees that something decisive had happened. He had behaved correctly in a critical situation. He had held his own. He had not failed. Involuntarily he righted himself in his seat as if he were suddenly free from a heavy burden, and the vibration of the plane sent shivers of delight through his body.

The mountains of Hurdal approached, and the two aircraft levelled out for a moment so that they might not go down too low. They saw nothing of the helicopter. But it probably did not matter; helicopters never seemed to feel at home in the neighbourhood of jets, and the pilot had probably heard the radio conversation and descended to a safe height at the bottom of the valley.

The controller took no chances. He called up the helicopter, and asked its position. There was no answer. The voice of the controller came sharp and impatient: "Helicopter 36—do you hear me? What is your position and height? Over."

"Hurdal, 500." The answer came quickly, but unwillingly.

The voice was Svein's.

CHAPTER FOURTEEN

All Clear

JUST before they reached the aerodrome Geir got a glimpse of the helicopter to the west of the aerodrome. It was moving slowly southwards, flying low. When he and Peter reached their parking place and shut off their engines it had disappeared behind the mountains towards Nittedalen.

Geir jumped out of his aircraft, and began walking towards

the dispersal hut. He stopped at the steps, sat down on the top step, and waited for Peter.

"Thank you for your help, Peter," he said.

"Oh, it was nothing." Peter smiled a little uncertainly. He put down his parachute, and stood with one foot on the bottom step, resting his elbow on his knee.

"Nothing?" said Geir. "You saved my aircraft, at any rate; twice, as a matter of fact."

Peter did not answer at once. He looked searchingly at Geir and tried to catch his eye. "What happened? How did it really begin?" he asked.

"I forgot the trim. I had trimmed to the left in the spiral on our way up, and let go of the stick to turn a switch. Then I flipped over before I could say knife."

"But you must have felt that the stick was badly trimmed?"

"Of course I felt it." Geir stood up and took his parachute under his arm. His voice was indifferent, a little *too* indifferent to be typical of him. It did not seem natural. "It is the sort of thing that happens only once in a lifetime. You sit and pull the stick, or cross the rudders, thinking of something else——"

He turned and went into the corridor. They pulled off their flying clothes and hung them up in the cupboards.

"See you later," said Geir, and opened the door to the flight commander's office.

"May I come in with you?"

"Of course."

Geir left the door open, sat down at the desk, and opened the report book, while Peter settled himself in a chair at the window, and gazed at an aircraft passing on its way to the runway. He rested his chin on one hand; there was a thoughtful frown between his eyes.

"Do you know what Svein was doing up there?" he asked, without turning round.

"No, why should I know? He often flies past here, doesn't he?"

"Do you think Svein would have flown past us if he had heard our radio conversation?"

"He couldn't have heard it," said Geir.

"Why not? He was on the same frequency as we were. when the controller called him up."

"Yes. That's rather odd."

"It was actually rather strange, too, that he was in our neighbourhood when we were just about to collide; don't you think so?"

Geir turned over the leaves of the report book. "Yes. . . . Oh yes, now you mention it."

Peter turned round abruptly. He heard the uncertainty in Geir's voice, and he thought there must be something more than appeared on the surface. There were too many circumstances fitting into each other. "Tell me what happened then," he said with a strange undertone in his voice.

"But I have."

Geir did not look up from the report book. He went on turning over the leaves, carefully scrutinising the entries here and there.

"Did anything special happen on the 3rd July?" asked Peter a little later.

"What did you say?"

"You're sitting there reading the report for the 3rd July."

"Oh, yes—er—er—yes, I am looking for something."

They were both silent. The air was heavy as before a storm. They were waiting for each other. Both knew that they must speak frankly, and get it over.

Geir closed the book.

"All right," he said heavily. "You have guessed right. I did it on purpose."

Peter grasped the arms of his chair, and stared at him as though he could scarcely believe it. "How *could* you?" he almost whispered.

"*Tja*," said Geir, looking very guilty. "Now that it is all over I can scarcely imagine myself. Taking all in all, it was not as simple as I thought. But, on the other hand, it was not so dangerous as *you* think. I did not cross your course—you must be quite clear about that. I did not take the actual chance of a collision. I only swerved over with crossed rudders, and I have been training for it for weeks."

Peter's face was half in shadow. He picked at a piece of rough nail and did not answer.

"You reacted correctly," said Geir helplessly.

Peter cleared his throat. "Did you expect me to do so?"

"I was absolutely certain that you would."

They were silent again. Peter studied his nail and Geir scraped at a blob of sealing-wax on the desk.

"Did anyone help you to plan this?" It was Peter who broke the silence.

"No. I did not dare tell Tangen. Don't dare now, either. This was *my* sideslip. I haven't made many."

"But Svein——?"

"Oh, yes, Svein knew; I told him about it. But how in the world . . ? Wait a moment."

Geir was thankful to get the conversation into another channel. He took up the telephone, and a moment later a voice answered: "Flying Control!" Geir looked quite exhausted. "This is Lieutenant Grand," he said. "On what task was the helicopter who passed a moment ago engaged?"

He held the telephone a little way from his ear, so that they could both hear the answer. "Don't know. He landed here this morning, and took off again about an hour later. When he took off he rang from Hangar 'C' and informed us that he was on his way north along the Hurdal Lake at 3,000 feet and would return to Rygge about an hour later. He said nothing about the task on which he was engaged."

"When did he take off?"

"Five minutes to nine."

"Thank you." Geir put back the receiver and they looked at each other quite disconcerted. "The same departure time as ours," said Geir, and tried an uncertain smile. "He must have listened to the radio as we ran the aircraft out to the starting place, and after that I suppose he followed our condensation trails."

Peter looked down and said nothing.

A few seconds passed before he was able to answer. First he cleared his throat, then opened his mouth, then shut it again, and finally stood up and went over to the window. When he spoke his voice was husky: "Then he wasn't as sure as you were?"

"No, I don't think he was." Geir tried to make his voice sound light. "But I was right in the end; at least, in a way."

"He too——"

"Yes!"

Suddenly they both began to laugh, shyly, as if they were strangers to each other. Peter put his hands into his pockets, and raised his shoulders.

"I don't know which of you is the worst," he said thickly. "You both seem to be very risky friends to have." He was silent for a moment. "Now and then it comes in useful," he added.

Geir coughed, and looked at his watch. "Shall we drive across to lunch?" he asked.

"What time is it?"

"A quarter past eleven."

"Then we've got plenty of time. Can't we walk for once in a while? Round the perimeter?"

"Of course!"

They came out into the sunshine, and followed the concrete strip eastwards. A nip in the air warned them that autumn was on its way, but the sky was high and free from cloud. When they were out of sight of the squadron area they put their hands in their pockets and cut down their speed. The corn that was cultivated between the taxi-strip and the runway hung on the frames and smelt good. A tractor dragging a fully-loaded cart drove out through the north gate.

"The summer will soon be over," said Geir.

"Yes, I suppose the weather will change any day now."

"But it's been a lovely summer."

"Yes, in many ways."

"I was thinking of the weather."

"Yes."

The soles of their shoes beat against the concrete.

"Geir?"

"Yes?"

"I have been very stupid. A bad comrade."

"Oh no; it's not as bad as all that."

"Bad enough, Geir. But you can count on it being different from now on, both on the ground and in the air."

"I know that. I know that, Peter."

They stopped in front of the runway crossing and waited while an aircraft came in to land. Then they went on.

"Geir?"

"Yes?"

"I have often wondered about one thing."

"What's that?"

"Well, I have wondered why none of us who fly can ever contemplate another occupation. Nearly everyone else longs for a change, or thinks he would like to try something new. But not us."

"No. You've got something there." Geir kicked a stone off the runway.

"What do you think is the reason for that?"

Geir thought a moment. "Oh, well, . . . all the things we experience, I suppose. We have variation enough without changing our job."

Peter looked disappointed. "Do you think that's all?"

"Oh no." Geir thought again for a moment. "No. If you want me to be more solemn about it, it's all right by me. I look at it this way. Flying gives something and demands something, like every job. What it gives you know as well as I do—excitement, joy of speed, for example; the feeling that the power of the aircraft is yours; or experiences such as when you jump straight from rain into sun, or climb at dusk and see a new sunrise, while the night becomes darker and darker beneath you. Those things are experiences that no one but an airman knows. You know what I mean; sometimes you feel inclined to pinch yourself to see whether you are dreaming or whether you are awake. Isn't that so?"

Peter nodded, and said nothing.

"Well. . . " Geir paused and looked rather worried. He fumbled for his words. "Well, that is what flying gives. You experience much that you would not miss for the world, but I don't think that is the most important part. That which means most is what flying *demands*—the whole of you, body, soul, and spirit, all you have of strength and ability. You simply can't give up flying, because it is, before anything else, a *challenge*."

They walked on silently.

Now and again a yellow leaf whirled down across the concrete from the adjoining forest. It crackled when they trod on it. Yes, summer was drawing to a close.

Notes on Jets and the Art of Flying Them

MILITARY flying units are known as squadrons. They are designated by a three-figure number; for example, 331 or 717. When speaking of the squadron one would say, "Three three one squadron", or "Seven one seven squadron."

There are, as a rule, about twenty-five planes to a squadron, thirty pilots, and over a hundred mechanics. It is led by a squadron commander, and among the pilots there are four flight commanders, each of whom leads his own flight, A, B, C, or D flight. In the air each flight consists of four planes, but generally a flight commander is responsible for more planes and pilots; for reserves are necessary, so that the squadron may always be able to operate at full strength. When the entire squadron flies, the Squadron Commander leads A-Flight.

The mechanics are commanded by the squadron's technical officer. There are two permanent mechanics for each plane, who do the daily inspections, and keep it in order. The other mechanics are specialists who work in the squadron's radio-, instrument-, and weapon-workshops.

Each squadron has a call-sign, which is used in conversations over the radio. If, for example, a squadron has the call-sign "Panther", the squadron commander is known as "Panther Leader". Each flight uses a colour in addition to the squadron's call-sign. In "Blue" flight the flight commander will be known as "Panther Blue Leader" or "Blue 1", and the other pilots as "Blue 2", "Blue 3", and "Blue 4". Furthermore, each has a personal call-sign which is used when he flies alone. It consists of the squadron's call-sign and a number; for example "Panther 14", which is pronounced "Panther one four".

There are various expressions used in flying which are

difficult for the uninitiated to understand without explanation. The most important are:

Aerobatics. The most usual aerobatics are the following:

Loop. The plane goes up, over on its back, and down again in a circle-like movement.

Roll. The plane rotates around its longitudinal axis.

Spin. The plane goes right down in a sharp spiral. The wing which lies inside the turn has less speed than the one that lies outside. The inner wing has, therefore, insufficient lifting power, and the plane is partly out of control. The cockpit lies inward in the turn.

Inverted Spin. The plane goes in a spiral as in an ordinary spin, but the cockpit lies outward in the turn. The pilot is pressed from his seat by both the centrifugal force and the force of gravitation, so that he is forced against his shoulder-straps with his head down.

Artificial Horizon. When a pilot is flying in cloud or in complete darkness he cannot distinguish up from down. If, for example, he goes into a loop, the centrifugal force presses him against his seat. The same thing happens if he goes into a steep turn. Thus, without instruments he does not know whether he is looping or turning, and without instruments he would sooner or later lose control of the plane. But the instruments help him. The most important of them is called the Artificial Horizon. A round plate with a little plastic aircraft in the middle is fixed to the instrument board. In front of and straight across the plate is a horizontal line which, with the help of a gyro, is kept absolutely still in relation to the earth. If the aircraft tilts, the plastic aircraft does so too, because it is attached to the plate. The horizon line, however, is kept parallel to the earth's horizon. The movement of the plastic aircraft in relation to the horizon line therefore shows the actual tilt in relation to the earth.

As long as the pilot keeps the plastic aircraft on the horizon line and with the wings parallel with it, he knows that he is flying straight forward at a constant height.

Bearings. When there is fog or low cloud on an aerodrome, many different methods are used in order to lead the pilot down to a height from which he can see the runway, and land with safety. Both radar and radio methods are employed. (1) With radar the aircraft can be detected through the clouds, and a radar operator on the ground can lead the pilot by telling him over the radio how he is to fly. (2) The majority of radio systems work by a cone of radio waves, which is sent out in the direction from which the plane is approaching the runway. The waves are received by special radio sets in the plane when it enters the cone—either as sound signals or by visual indications on instruments in the cockpit. In this way the pilot can either hear or see whether he is in the cone, which will lead him straight to the runway. He can also find out if he is in the middle of the cone; that is, if he is over, under, or to the right or left of its centre line. (3) Passage through the clouds with the help of radio bearings is a simpler method which jets very often use. The pilot presses the radio button and gives his call-sign. A homing aerial on the ground is pulled round until the sound from the pilot's radio has almost disappeared. Then the operator knows that the aerial is right across the direction towards the plane, and a bearing plate shows which course he must give the pilot. The course is given in degrees— east is 90 degrees, south 180 degrees, west 270 degrees, and north 360 degrees.

Black Out. When the plane is put into a sharp turn or loop, the centrifugal force presses the pilot against his seat. He has to brace his muscles to keep himself upright. The centrifugal force also acts on the pilot's blood, which is pressed downward and streams away from his brain. This causes loss of vision, and the pilot becomes more or less blind as long as he is affected by the centrifugal force. He has a "black-out".

Condensation Trails. The water-vapour in the warm jet stream condenses when it emerges into the cold air. In this way it becomes a cloud which lies like a strip behind the plane. The strips are produced only when the temperature and the humidity of the atmosphere are suitable for it, and generally only at a great height.

Crash Commission. After a crash a commission is always appointed which questions witnesses and examines the wreck in order to find out how the crash happened. Usually investigation results in new rules and regulations, or in alterations of the plane's or the pilot's outfit, in the hope of avoiding similar accidents in future.

Ejection Seat. Modern jet aircraft go so fast that it is impossible to bale out in the usual way. Therefore the pilot's seat has a discharge mechanism attached to it. When he presses a switch a charge goes off, and the whole chair is thrown out of the cockpit with great speed. As soon as the chair is clear of the plane, another mechanism opens the belt with which the pilot is fastened to the chair, and he is then freed from it. The parachute can now be opened in the usual way by the pilot. But, if he does not do so, it is opened automatically by a barometer (which measures the height) and a clockwork mechanism. The barometer sets the mechanism going as soon as the height is below 14,000 feet. Down to that the pilot falls freely, but when he reaches this height the clockwork mechanism begins to work, and the parachute opens after three seconds. The reason why it is not expedient to allow the parachute to open higher up is that it is too cold, and there is too little oxygen, there. It is important for the pilot to come down to a lower height as quickly as possible.

Jet aircraft. Propelled aircraft are, as is well known, driven through the air by airscrews. Jets are forced forward. The air that streams in through the gap in the nose is sucked into a gas turbine and compressed with the help of a turbine wheel. The air is supplied with fuel in the combustion chamber, and the mixture is ignited. The compressed combustion gases force their way out through the opening in the tail. As a result the plane is driven forward in the same way as a garden hose is pressed backward if it is lying on the ground when the water is turned on.

Machmeter. Velocity of the air (about 360 yards per second or 750 miles per hour at sea level is a border-line that only special aircraft can surmount. The boundary is called the Sound Barrier. When an aircraft approaches the sound barrier, it finds tremendous air resistance, and aircraft which are not specially built for so great or greater speed are destroyed either before they meet the sound barrier or when they actually meet it. It is, therefore, more important to know how great is the speed in relation to the velocity of sound than to know how many miles an hour the plane is doing.

The velocity of sound is not always the same. The colder the air the lower the velocity. At a great height, therefore, it is lower than just above the ground. The machmeter measures the speed of the plane in relation to the speed of sound in the air which surrounds it at that moment. Mach 1 is the velocity of sound, Mach 2 is double the velocity of sound, Mach 0·8 is $\frac{8}{10}$ of the velocity of sound.

Oxygen Mask. The higher the pilot rises the less oxygen is in the air that he breathes. For great heights he must, therefore, obtain extra oxygen through the oxygen mask. If the oxygen system fails at a great height, the pilot faints, and only comes to himself as he descends to air that is richer in oxygen.

Pilot Investigation Board. Jet flying demands that the pilot's nerves and physique shall be in top form. If there is a doubt whether a pilot is the complete master of his plane, the Investigation Board becomes active. It consists of the wing commander, the station medical officer, the station commander, and a pilot of the same rank as the one under discussion. The Board estimates the capabilities of the pilot, and makes a recommendation to the Commander-in-Chief. There are three possible decisions—that the pilot may continue to fly, that he shall be given a period of rest in a different type of work, or that he shall be permanently grounded.

Pressurised Cockpit. At great heights the pressure of the air is so low that it is harmful to the pilot. At really great heights his blood may reach boiling point. The planes have, therefore, a pressurised cockpit. When the pressure regulator is turned on a compressor pumps air into the cabin and keeps the pressure constant. The pressure is regulated by a barostat.